TO LIVE AND DRAW IN L.A.

Now living in Los Angeles with
former Navy SEAL Nick Reno,
artist Perry Foster comes to the rescue
of elderly and eccentric Horace Daly,
the legendary film star of such horror
classics as *Why Won't You Die, My Darling?*

Horace owns the famous,
but now run-down, Hollywood hotel
Angel's Rest, rumored to be haunted.

But as far as Perry can tell,
the scariest thing about Angel's Rest
is the cast of crazy tenants—
one of whom seems determined to bring down
the final curtain on Horace—
and anyone else who gets in the way.

THE GHOST HAD AN EARLY CHECK-OUT

December 2018

Copyright (c) 2018 by Josh Lanyon

Edited by Keren Reed

Cover and book design by Kevin Burton Smith

ISBN: 978-1-794177-96-3

Published in the United States of America

JustJoshin Publishing, Inc.

3053 Rancho Vista Blvd.

Suite 116

Palmdale, CA 93551

www.joshlanyon.com

This is a work of fiction. Any resemblance to persons living or dead is entirely coincidental.

To Alison —
Happy reading!
Josh

THE GHOST HAD AN EARLY CHECK-OUT

JOSH LANYON

VELLICHOR BOOKS

An imprint of JustJoshin Publishing, Inc.

To Sabine, with love and thanks.

CHAPTER ONE

"**H**elp! Help!"

A scream split the autumn afternoon.

Perry, precariously perched on the twisted limb of a dying oak tree, lost his balance, dropped his sketch pad, and nearly followed its fluttering descent into the tall, yellowing grass growing on the other side of the chain-link fence that was supposed to keep people like himself from trespassing on the grounds of the former Angel's Rest hotel.

The voice was thin and hoarse, sexless. There was no sign of anyone, but the cries bounced off the chipped gargoyles, crumbling stairs, and broken fountains, echoed off the pointed towers and mansard rooftops of the eight-story building. The ravens flocking on the east tower window ledge took flight.

Recovering his balance, Perry scooted along the thick branch until he was safely over the barbed top of the fence, and then jumped down into the waist-high weeds and grass.

"Help!"

Heart pounding, Perry ran toward the voice—or at least where he guessed the voice was coming from. He still couldn't see anyone.

This back section of the property had never been land-scaped. Thirsty scrub oaks, bramble bushes, webs of potentially ankle-snapping weeds covered a couple of sunbaked acres. It was unseasonably hot for late October.

When he reached the wall of towering, mostly dead hedges, he covered his mouth and nose with the crook of his arm and shoved his way through, trying not to inhale dust or pollen.

Small, sharp dried leaves whispered as they scratched his bare skin, crumbling against his clothes. He scraped through and found himself in the ruins of the actual hotel garden.

Which meant he was…*where* in relation to the voice?

Without his leafy vantage point, he had no clue. Rusted lanterns hung from withered tree branches. A couple of short stone staircases led nowhere. An ornate, but oxidized, iron patio chair was shoved into the hedge, and a little farther on, an overturned patio table lay on its back, four legs sticking straight up out of the tall weeds like a dead animal. A black and white checkered cement square was carpeted in broken branches and debris. A giant gameboard? More likely an outdoors dance floor.

Too bad there was no time to get some of this derelict grandeur down on paper…

Finally, he spotted an overgrown path leading through a pair of moribund Japanese cedars—so ossified they looked like wood carvings—and jogged on toward the hotel.

The voice had fallen silent.

Perry slowed to an uneasy stop, listening. His breathing was the loudest sound in the artificial glade. Should he go on? You couldn't—shouldn't—ignore a cry for help, but maybe the emergency was over?

Or maybe the emergency had gotten so much worse, whoever had been yelling was now unconscious.

Far overhead, the tops of the trees made a distant rustling sound, though there was no breeze down here in the petrified forest. He could see broken beer bottles along the path, cigarette butts, and something that appeared to be a used condom.

Ugh.

The hotel would be a magnet for vagrants and delinquents alike. His heart still pounded in that adrenaline rush, and he was breathing hard, but it was simply normal exertion. He was uneasy, of course, but there was no reason he couldn't go on. *He* was not the one in distress.

One thing for sure: Nick would not hesitate one instant to offer help to someone in need—although he also would not be crazy about Perry charging into potential trouble.

Perry continued down the path. Actually, it was more of a trail, and it ended abruptly at the top of the terraced hillside. There didn't seem to be another way down, so he just plowed through the desiccated brush, trying not to lose his footing amid the loose earth and broken stones.

At last—well, it felt like *at last*, but it was probably no more than two or three minutes—he reached the bottom of the first of three wide, shallow flights of steps, which surely led to the back entrance of the hotel.

Now what?

Aside from his own footfalls and raspy breathing, it was eerily silent.

He began to feel a little foolish.

Had he misunderstood those cries? Maybe he'd been fooled by the noise of a bunch of kids roughhousing. Maybe what he'd heard had been the rantings of a crazy homeless person. There was a lot of that in LA.

Maybe there *had* been real trouble, but the situation was now resolved.

He'd been sketching Angel's Rest for the past week—ever since he'd seen photos of it during his friend Dorian's exhibition the previous Saturday—so he knew that technically there were several tenants (or maybe just squatters) in the old hotel. In which case, maybe someone had already rushed to the rescue.

Then again, maybe someone was dying while he stood here trying to make his mind up.

"Just do it," Perry muttered, and started up the steps toward the hotel.

The back entrance to the building had to be up there somewhere. The pool was over to the left behind another wall of brown hedges, but it was nearly empty, and if someone had fallen off the side of that, they would probably be dead. The conservatory, vines growing out the top and broken glass winking in the sun, was to the right behind still more hedges. That was another potential deathtrap, but he'd never seen anyone out there either. In fact, he had never seen anyone outside the hotel at all. The only reason he knew the place was inhabited was because of the scattered lights that went on at dusk and the occasional scent of cooking food on the breeze.

Halfway up the first flight, a scrape of sound—footsteps on pavement—reached him. Perry raised his head as three figures crested the top. He froze. His breath caught. His heart seemed to tumble through his chest as he stared in disbelief.

Three figures. They wore long black capes and skeleton masks. They carried swords.

Swords.

It was...unexpected.

Okay, fucking terrifying. Skeleton men carrying swords was definitely an unexpected *and* unnerving sight.

His thoughts were jumbled. Was someone filming a movie? Pretty much everywhere you went in LA someone was filming something. Was this a trial run for Halloween? The holiday was only two days away. Were they bank robbers? He had some experience of bank robbers, so the thought wasn't as random as it might seem.

Was he dreaming?

No. He could feel the October sun beating down on his head, smell the dust and pollen rising from the cement. Perspiration trickled slowly down his spine to his tailbone. His heart banged against his ribs. His breathing was too fast and getting shallow. He was definitely not dreaming.

The fact that it was broad daylight made it worse somehow. Surreal. The blaze of sunlight lancing off pale stone, the dark fireball shadows thrown by the towering palm trees, the tall black-and-white figures sweeping down the stairs toward him...

It should have been a dream. If *felt* like a dream.

"*Hey!*" Perry shouted. He was a little surprised by his ferocity. Mostly that was him trying to get past his apprehension with a show of force. Plus, he had to say *something*.

The skeleton men were also running and did not notice Perry until he yelled. By then they were almost on top of him. They didn't speak, but he had an impression of surprised alarm. Being an artist, he automatically paid attention to movement, to body language, to facial expressions. Well, there was no facial expression on those grinning, gaping skeleton faces, but three different sets of body language revealed varying degrees of shock. One of the skeletons veered left, the other veered right.

The middle skeleton, who was a few steps behind the other two, raised his sword and charged straight at Perry.

No. This is not happening. This cannot be happening...

But the point of that sword was headed straight for his chest.

For a stricken instant, Perry couldn't seem to process, but getting skewered for trespassing was not something he wanted to explain to Nick, and the thought galvanized him. Instinctively, he dived and tackled the other around his legs.

The skeleton man pitched forward, his hand locking on the collar of Perry's T-shirt, dragging Perry with him. Perry ducked his head protectively against his shoulder, still trying to hang on to his assailant.

Hard muscles bunched beneath his hands. The other grunted but did not call out as they bumped their way down the steps, turning over and over. As they rolled, Perry got flashes of blue sky, sparkling bits of broken limestone step, a razor-burned throat, brown leaves, clouds, scuffed army boots...

He could smell BO and cigarettes and musty wool.

The sword clattered noisily in front of them. It sounded like wood.

He'd heard Nick talk about how time seemed to both speed up and move in slow motion when you were in a fight, and that was exactly how it felt. He had time to register the little details of sight, smell, sound, but they went past in a confused rush, like a racing freight train.

Nick had been right about something else too. He was already exhausted. His heart clamored in his chest, his lungs burned, his muscles shook. Punches thumped down on his shoulder and back, but that pain felt more distant than his instant and immediate physical distress.

What the fuck was he going to do with this asshole once they reached the bottom?

The skeleton man tried to knee Perry in the groin, tried to bang his head against the steps. Perry, his hands otherwise engaged, tried to head-butt him. His forehead collided with the guy's chin.

Thunk.

Ouch.

Bad decision. It seemed pretty straightforward when demonstrated by Nick, but was not so simple in execution. Slamming his forehead into the other's masked face made him see stars—while having no visible effect on his opponent.

But it also knocked some sense into Perry.

He did not want to land at the feet of the other two skeleton men. That would not be a good plan.

He let go of the man's cape and costume and tried to stop his own rolling descent, which…momentum was not his friend. He did manage to shove the guy off and come to a stop. Shakily, he started to pick himself up, watching warily as the other tumbled the rest of the way to the foot of the steps.

Perry's arms wobbled, and he was having difficulty catching his breath. That was fatigue, not asthma, although with the number of stressors he was experiencing, that situation might change any minute.

He had worse problems. His sprawled foe crawled around on his knees, scrabbling for his fallen sword.

Perry's stomach did an unhappy flop. Really? More? He was not ready for round two.

As the skeleton's hand closed around the hilt, he was dragged to his feet by his cohorts, one of whom panted, "Forget it, man. Leave him."

It seemed touch-and-go, but then the skeleton man jabbed his hand at Perry. Even without words, the message was clearly, *You're dead!*

Before he could make good on the threat, he was hustled away, and the three took off running, disappearing into the overgrown jungle of crumbling rosebushes and run-amuck ornamental grasses.

For a few shocked moments Perry stared after them, not moving, simply trying to catch his breath. What the hell had just happened?

At the sound of low moans coming from overhead, he pushed upright and limped hurriedly up the stairs.

There was an arched entrance at the top of the steps. The archway led into the ruins of a walled garden. Shriveled vines hung like threadbare draperies. In the center of the courtyard was a cracked, dirty fountain, ringed by curved benches. On the far side of the yard was another doorway leading to a terrace with tall Palladian-style doors, which must open into what would once have been the hotel foyer.

An elderly man slumped against the base of the fountain, clutching his midriff and groaning quietly. He wore blue jeans and a white shirt. His hair was silver and shoulder-length. His beard was also silver and worn Van Dyke style.

Perry stumbled forward, expecting to see blood gushing from beneath the clasped hands. "Are you all right?" he gulped. "Did they get you?"

The old man's eyes shot open, and he half sat up. To Perry's relief, there did not appear to be any sign of gore on his hands or clothes.

"Who are *you*?" The voice sounded much stronger than the moans indicated. "Where did you come from?"

"Perry Foster. I heard you yelling for help."

"You…"

"Are you badly hurt?" Perry asked. "Do you need an ambulance?"

The old man was staring at him as though Perry was an apparition. He had very blue eyes. Not the deep marine blue of Nick's. A pale, glittery blue like gemstones. With that high, elegant bone structure, he had probably been very, very handsome in his youth. He was still striking even as he gawked wide-eyed at Perry.

"Did you *see* them?" he demanded.

"Yes. I saw them. Do you want me to call someone? Should I call the police?"

"You *saw* them?"

They would have been hard to miss, wouldn't they?

"Yes," Perry said. "We ran into each other on the stairs."

Still clutching his midsection, the old man struggled to stand. Perry went to his aid. A bony hand fastened on his shoulder, and the old man peered into his eyes.

"Who *are* you?" he asked again.

"Perry," Perry repeated. "Perry Foster."

"Do I know you?"

"Well, no."

The old man continued to peer at him. "Perry, you said?"

"Perry Foster."

"And you say you saw them. What did you see?"

Old though he was, he had a beautiful, deep voice. A commanding voice. A trained voice?

Perry answered obediently, "I saw three figures—male; at least, I'm sure two of them were male—dressed up in skeleton costumes and capes. They had swords." He recalled the clatter of the sword bouncing down the steps. "Wooden swords, I think."

"Oh, thank God." The old man shut his eyes and swayed. "*Thank. God.*"

"Here, you better sit down." Perry helped him to one of the marble benches. He was tall, taller than Perry, but willowy. All at once he seemed very frail.

The old man rested his face in his hands and shook his head. Then he raised his head. "You don't understand." He shook his head again. Tears shimmered in his eyes. He covered his face.

Perry looked around for help, but there was no sign of anyone. He waited for a couple of moments while the old guy tried to compose himself.

"Is there someone inside?" Perry asked finally. "Is there someone I can get for you?"

"No, no." The old man wiped his eyes without self-consciousness. "How did you get here, Perry? Where did you come from?"

Oh, *that*. Perry grimaced. The moment of truth. "Well, you see… I've been sketching Angel's Rest. The building."

There was no comprehension on the face in front of him—and why would there be?

Perry persisted. "Maybe I should have asked permission. I didn't really think about it until now. There's an oak tree in the back on the other side of the property line. The branches grow over the fence, and I was sitting up there."

The old man frowned. "What do you mean you were sketching the building? Why?"

"Because it's…beautiful. The bones of the structure, I mean. The architecture."

Instead of replying, the old man once more dropped his head to his hands.

Perry glanced back at the tall, dark windows of the hotel. Why was no one coming out? How was it possible that no one had heard any of this commotion?

The man lifted his head and glared at Perry with unexpectedly hard blue eyes.

"If you're an artist, where are your paints or pencils? Where is your easel or your sketchbook?"

The sudden suspicion was startling. Why would he lie about sketching the property? After all, he could have come up with all kinds of fake excuses for being on the grounds, if that's what the old guy was hinting at.

Perry said, "I dropped my gear when you yelled."

"I see. Then it will still be where you left it." The distrust was still there, bright and shining.

"Yes. It should still be lying there in the grass." Then again, the way things were going? Perry added, "I hope."

"Show me."

Perry stepped back warily as his rescuee rose. "Okay, but wouldn't it make more sense to call the police?"

The old man gave a short, bitter laugh. "Would it? No. Show me where you left your things when you raced to my rescue."

Not that Perry was looking for a big thank-you, but the hint of sarcasm in "when you raced to my rescue" was strange and troubling. So too was the other's obvious paranoia. An already very weird situation seemed to be getting weirder by the minute.

"Sure." Perry turned to lead the way. He was suddenly, painfully conscious of his own bumps and bruises. He hadn't fallen far, but it had been a hard landing. He'd banged his elbow, his knee, his shoulder. He was very lucky he hadn't broken anything.

They walked down the three flights of steps in silence, but when Perry started toward the terraced hillside, the old man said, "What are you doing? There's a walkway right here."

Sure enough, beneath the dead leaves and pine needles, a brick walk wound through the black iron pickup sticks of what had once been an ornate gate. Perry hadn't noticed the walkway in his earlier haste.

"Oh. Right. Okay." He changed course obligingly. The old man gave him a sideways look.

"I suppose you think I'm ungrateful?"

"Well, I guess you're pretty shaken up." He felt pretty shaken himself, and he hadn't been the target of that attack.

The old man made an unappeased sound. "I have to wonder. How would you happen to be here at just the right moment to see them? Hm? *That* timing is a little *too* convenient."

Perry tried to read his face, tried to make sense of the open disbelief. Not just disbelief. Antipathy. Like the old guy thought he was…what? What was he implying? That Perry had been with the skeleton men? That he was part of a gang of Halloween-costumed hooligans who went around beating up old people?

"I've been here all week," Perry said.

"All week? You've been trespassing all week?"

Old people could be cranky, that was a fact. Perry tried to hang on to his patience. "If I *was* trespassing on your property, it was only today when I heard you yelling."

"Yet how *could* you hear anything from this distance?"

This was getting kind of ridiculous. "I guess the breeze was blowing in the right direction."

The old man made an unconvinced noise.

Well, he could think what he liked. He seemed as unhurt as he was ungrateful, so really Perry's responsibility—assuming he had any in this situation—was at an end. He'd grab his gear and show this old coot that he was exactly what he said he was, and then climb back over the fence and head home. He had plenty of sketches of Angel's Rest by now. He could paint from those. Or find another project. He wouldn't be returning here again, that was for sure.

The brick path took them past the checkerboard dance floor and up the path with the broken bottles and trash. The old man made a sound of disgust as he noted the discarded condom.

"Kind of a weird place for romance," Perry offered. It was not in his nature to hang on to irritation.

"Hm."

Though Perry's companion was also limping, he didn't really move like an old person. He *was* old, though. Seventy at least. Perry had spent a lot of time with elderly people, both when he worked at the library in Fox Run and when he'd lived on the Alston Estate. He was used to their quirks and general crankiness. The last of his exasperation faded.

"Have you lived here a long time?" he asked.

The old man gave him look of disbelief and did not deign to answer.

Perry sighed.

They didn't speak again until they trudged across the barren back of the property and reached the oak tree. Perry hunted through the dry grass and found his sketch pad. He brushed the foxtails out of the pages and handed it over to his companion. He pointed up into the overhanging branches.

"You can see my backpack up there. Leaning against that Y in the trunk."

The old man, flipping brusquely through the pages of Perry's sketchbook, did not look up. "My God." He paused at a sketch of a raven perched on the sill of one of the tower windows. "Where did you learn to draw like this?"

"Art classes and stuff."

He did look up then. "No." Pale blue eyes met Perry's solemnly. "This is…this is a gift. This isn't training."

"Well, a lot of it is training."

He continued to stare as though seeing Perry clearly for the first time. "It's a gift from the gods," he pronounced.

Oh-kay, *that* was a little dramatic.

"Yeah, but I don't really…" Believe in gods? Believe in talent without training? Believe you're entirely sane, Mr. Angel's Rest?

"It's the Muse," insisted Mr. Angel's Rest. "It's fire from heaven."

Fire from heaven? What did that even mean? This oldster would have been right at home on the Alston Estate with little old Miss Dembecki and creepy Mr. Teagle.

Perry said politely, "I guess some of it is aptitude."

The good news was he no longer seemed to be suspected of being in league with the skeleton men.

As though reading his thoughts, the old man flipped closed the sketchbook and offered his hand. "I'm Horace Daly. I want to thank you for what you did for me earlier, and I'm sorry I wasn't more…gracious."

"That's okay," Perry began. He was hoping Horace wasn't planning on keeping his sketchbook. "Do y—"

"No, it's really not," Horace said earnestly. "But it's difficult to explain without sounding completely mad."

Mad? Horace Daly seemed to have quite the dramatic turn of phrase. But then he was living in a mostly abandoned hotel and had just been attacked by three guys in skeleton costumes, so maybe drama was his default?

Perry opened his mouth to…well, he wasn't sure what. Ask if Horace needed help getting back home? Ask if Horace wanted to file a police report perhaps? Because really, that's what they should be doing right now. Phoning the cops. The longer they waited, the less chance they had of—

Who was he kidding? They had zero chance of catching Horace's attackers at this point.

Horace was still watching him with that blazing-eyed intensity. When he stared like that, he *almost*…sort of…looked familiar.

Had he seen Horace before? Where? Why did he have the weird inkling it had been in church? Perry hadn't been to church since he'd left his parents' home nearly two years ago—and he was pretty sure Horace was no Presbyterian.

Horace, still following his own thoughts, pronounced in that grand, grave manner, "You see, Perry, someone is trying to kill me."

CHAPTER TWO

It was after eleven by the time Nick got home.

The apartment was dark and silent. It smelled of paint and linseed oil, which was how home smelled now. It would not smell like cooking because Perry did not bother to cook when Nick was not around for meals. It was a question whether he even bothered to eat.

Nick quietly set his bag down and turned on the living-room light. God, it was good to be back. He looked around approvingly. The room was comfortably furnished. His old blue sofa was positioned against one wall. Two small end tables they'd picked up at a Goodwill store sat at either end. The tables were topped with matching alabaster lamps that Perry assured him were terrific finds. Maybe. Nick had doubts about the antiquated wiring, but Perry loved them, so he'd bought the lamps. Nick's framed seascape hung on the opposite wall. A tall mahogany bookshelf, another Goodwill find, held Perry's paperbacks and his vintage clock. They were using an old trunk for their coffee table. Most of the remaining available space was taken up with Perry's canvases—those that were either on their way out to galleries and local shops or on their way back.

Everything appeared neat and tidy and in its place. Everything but Perry.

A quick glance in the bedroom verified that he was not in. Nick swallowed his disappointment. It was unusual for Perry to go to bed before midnight, and he hadn't known Nick was heading back to LA—Nick hadn't wanted to let him down in case things didn't wrap up on schedule—however, a survey of the apartment made it clear that not only was Perry not there, he hadn't been home since breakfast.

His rinsed cereal bowl sat in the sink. A box of Froot Loops sat on the breakfast counter. Perry teased Nick for being a neat freak, but he also did his best to accommodate those fifteen years of military regimen and order.

Nick stared at the red and white cereal bowl with a sinking feeling.

There were any number of benign explanations for why Perry wasn't home. He could be out with friends. He wasn't exactly a party animal, but he had made friends in art school, and he did hang out with them occasionally. He wouldn't have left a note because he wasn't expecting to see Nick until Sunday evening at the earliest.

He could have gone to a movie.

There were less benign possibilities too.

He could be stranded somewhere. That piece of junk car of his was always breaking down.

He could have had a severe asthma attack and landed in the hospital. Although, fortunately, he was so much better now that he was on those controller medications, an attack wasn't the concern it once would have been. LA's smog wasn't great for him, but it had been months since he'd had a real flare-up.

Nick listened to the sound of traffic outside the apartment as he continued to uneasily study Perry's cereal bowl. The streets were never silent here. At three o'clock in the morning, you could still hear the rush of the nearby freeway.

Well, it was a trade-off. Peace and quiet in exchange for a real job for him and a decent art school for Perry.

Unbidden, another thought slithered into his brain: *he could have met someone.*

What the hell? Where was that thought coming from? It wasn't the first time either. He rejected it instantly, impatiently. For God's sake. Perry wasn't home to greet him, and his thoughts jumped *there*?

It wasn't like he was even the jealous type. He knew Perry loved him, and God knew he loved Perry. More than he'd ever imagined he could love anyone. He trusted Perry.

But there was that ten-year age gap and the fact that Perry had never been exposed to so many other gay men before the move to LA.

Bullshit. Working all these goddamned divorce cases was what put the thought in his head.

That said, he'd have to be blind not to notice the way other guys responded to Perry—or the way Perry responded to finally getting some appreciative male attention. Meaning only that Perry's blushing confusion at being flirted with was touching.

And the kid was alone a lot. It couldn't be helped. Nick was low man on the totem pole, and most of the out-of-town and late-night gigs fell to him. Fair enough. He was grateful for the job and beyond grateful at the possibility that he might even be made a partner eventually. But it meant Perry was on his own in the big bad city a lot of the time.

And so what? Whatever was keeping Perry out at this time of night, it was not some illicit affair. Whatever. The job was what it was, and what it mostly was, was adulterous spouses and fraudulent insurance claims. He was lucky to have it. But. Not exactly why he'd become a Navy SEAL.

But then, he wasn't a SEAL anymore.

Nick was brooding over this, staring out the window over the kitchen sink at the smog-dimmed stars, when he heard the smothered sound of Perry's cough outside the apartment door. He stepped out of the kitchen as Perry's key turned the lock.

Perry opened the door, clearly surprised to find the lights on. His thin, pointy face lit up as he spotted Nick. "Hey, you're home!"

Nick retorted, "One detective per family is e—" but the rest of it was cut off as Perry launched himself. Nick's arms automatically locked around him, and his mouth came down hard on Perry's eager one.

What *was* it about Perry? He was cute enough, sure. Medium height, lanky, boyish-looking. His hair was blond and spiky. His eyes were big and brown and as long-lashed as a cartoon character's. In this town where two out of every three guys looked like they were trying out for a role in a major motion picture, Perry was almost strikingly ordinary. Maybe that was it. The fact that Perry didn't look like everyone else. That he didn't *act* like everyone else.

It was funny, though, because Perry was almost the complete opposite of what Nick had always thought was his type. Not that he had really thought of himself as having a *type*—beyond wanting someone with a penis.

Even after ten months, that unstinting…what the hell would you call it? *Sweetness* sounded too sappy, but there was something so honest, so generous in Perry's responses. It made Nick's heart feel too big for his chest. Closed his throat so that he could rarely say the things he wanted to say, things that Perry deserved to hear.

I love you. It scares me how much I love you.

Instead, he said gruffly, "Where the hell have you been at this hour?"

Perry didn't seem to hear the gruffness. His wide brown eyes smiled guilelessly up into Nick's. "I was sketching—"

He had to stop, though, starting to wheeze. He threw an apologetic look at Nick and dug out his rescue inhaler. He took a couple of quick puffs while Nick watched, frowning.

This was not good. He didn't like the sudden alarming reappearance of coughing and wheezing. He put a hand on Perry's shoulder. Under Nick's tutelage, Perry had built up some muscle, but he had not really put on much weight. His shoulders were still bony, his collarbones sharp.

"You okay?"

Perry put the inhaler away—he didn't like using it in front of Nick. As if he thought Nick looked down on him for it?

He said, "It was so dusty up there!"

"Where? Where've you been?" Nick hoped he didn't sound as accusatory as he did to his own ears.

"I drove up to Angel's Rest."

"Where?"

"That old hotel in the hills. Remember at Dorian's exhibition last Saturday? The 1920s hotel in those photos?"

"The abandoned place on Laurel Canyon?"

Jesus fucking Christ. He remembered Perry had seemed fascinated by those photos. But hiking around those hills on his own? Anything could happen to him, from being bit by a rattlesnake to running into some crazed homeless person.

Nick didn't let any of that show on his face. That was one
thing he had decided early on. He was not going to undermine
Perry's confidence or self-resilience with his own fears. Perry
was not his child, he was his partner. Physically frail or not, he
was a grown man.

"Right," Perry said quickly, as though he sensed everything Nick was determined not to say. "Only it's not abandoned.
Well, not completely."

Now, studying him more closely in the lamplight, Nick
noticed Perry's T-shirt was smeared with dust and torn at the
collar. And—more alarming—his knuckles were scraped and
cut.

Perry said, "Anyway, I'm sorry I'm late. I didn't know
you'd be back tonight. I bought pork chops for when you got
home."

"Were you in a *fight*?"

Perry's eyelashes flicked up guiltily. "Kind of."

"*Kind of?*"

Nick felt as winded as if Perry had punched *him*. Trying to
picture him in a fight was... Well, yes, Nick had been showing
him some moves, tried to prepare him a little in case he ever
had to defend himself, but still, Perry in a *fight*?

"I've got a lot to tell you," Perry said. "Should I cook the
pork chops?"

"I'll fix us something to eat. You talk."

In the kitchen Nick grabbed two bottles of beer from the
fridge, uncapped them, handing one to Perry and taking a long
swallow from his own. He came up for air and exhaled. He'd
needed that.

"How did the job go?" Perry asked, watching him.

"The usual. It was okay. I want to hear about your week."

Nick dug the package of pork chops out of the fridge while Perry told him about sketching Angel's Rest over the past few days—Nick hanging on to his patience while Perry was momentarily distracted by his enthusiasm for crumbling architecture and light and shadow—before finally describing hearing someone yelling for help from the hotel grounds.

Nick clenched his jaw on his instinctive protest. Of course Perry would respond. Of course he would try to help. It was the right thing to do, and by God, Nick was not going to try to tell him otherwise—although the sight of Perry sitting there with his torn T-shirt, bruised knuckles, and shining eyes worried the hell out of him.

While he prepared the pork chops, he heard out the whole ridiculous but still worrying story of men in skeleton costumes with wooden swords—and he was both proud and aghast that Perry had charged into the middle of that.

Perry chattered on, barely touching his own beer.

"He said his name was Horace Daly. He used to be an actor. He lives at the hotel. It's not a hotel anymore, though. Now it's sort of like apartments. Kind of like the Alston Estate really. Only—"

"Horace Daly," Nick interrupted. "The actor. I remember him."

"Yeah? I didn't recognize his name when he introduced himself, but I did sort of recognize his face."

"I thought he was dead."

"No. He's pretty old, but he seems spry. He's retired now, of course. You should see that place, Nick. He's got a bunch of movie memorabilia everywhere. You walk down a corridor, and suddenly you see a life-sized mummy standing in the shadows. Or a chopped off head sitting on a table. All these props from his films. There's a gibbet in the old ballroom. The real things they used in his movies, not replicas. At one time Horace thought maybe he could turn part of the hotel into a museum." Perry's eyes shone with enthusiasm, the artist in him no doubt getting off on the workmanship that went into creating realistic-looking skeletons and ghouls or whatever it was Daly kept in his closet.

Nick said, "Right. He was in all those old horror flicks. *Night of the Blue Witch*, *Seven Brides for Seven Demons*, *Sex and the Single Ghoul*."

"My parents wouldn't let me watch that stuff." Perry's expression was one of brooding regret.

Nick bit back a grin. "No, well. So, Daly is still around and lives in a not-quite-abandoned hotel?"

"Exactly. He owns the property. He rents the suites out to regular tenants." Perry amended, "Well, maybe *regular* isn't the word. I met a couple of them. But he's got about seven people renting from him."

"Huh," said Nick, noncommittal.

Perry's big brown eyes—wide with worry and concern—rose to his. "Horace thinks someone's trying to kill him."

"To kill him," Nick repeated. "He actually told you he thinks someone is trying to kill him?"

Perry nodded. "He says it's not the first time he's been attacked, but no one ever believed him because he's never had a witness before."

Several comments leaped to mind. Nick nobly squashed them all.

Perry was continuing his own line of thought. "He thinks it might be a crazed fan or someone like that. Someone who saw his movies and kind of lost it."

"So…like a movie critic?" Nick was teasing, but he didn't like this at all. Perry had seen the guys dressed up in skeleton costumes, so Horace wasn't making that part up, but the rest of it sounded pretty sketchy. Speaking as someone in the PI biz, homicides weren't really all that common. Not even in LA.

Perry made a face and laughed, but he continued to watch Nick in that serious, hopeful way as though he imagined Nick might have an instant solution to old Horace's problems.

"Why would someone want to knock Horace off?" Nick asked. "I mean, assuming it's not a crazed fan out to get him."

"But that's it. He's sure it *is* a crazed fan or a stalker. Someone confusing the movies with real life. He said for years he's been getting weird, threatening letters." Perry bit his lip, thinking. "He's hiding something, though."

Nick studied him. The funny thing about Perry was that despite his lack of worldly experience, he had good instincts about people. Reluctantly, he asked, "Why do you think so?"

Perry gave a little shake of his head. "I don't know. He's frightened. That's real. He does believe someone is trying to kill him." He said slowly, "What I think he's lying about is not knowing *why*."

"It would be in the letters, wouldn't it?"

"I guess. Horace said he didn't keep the letters."

Nick considered that piece of information. It might be the truth. It might be that Horace had the letters but didn't want anyone to see them. It might be that there never were any letters. He said, "I can tell you the usual reasons people kill. They want something someone else has. Usually money or sex."

"What about revenge?" Perry asked.

"I'm not saying it doesn't happen. Just that it's not nearly as common in real life as it is on TV."

"I don't think either money or sex would apply in Horace's case."

Probably not. Nick was having trouble believing in any scenario where an aging and long-forgotten film star would have a murderous stalker.

"But you think revenge would?"

"Er...no. But by process of elimination..."

Nick sighed inwardly. Thanks to true-crime TV, everybody thought they were a PI. Even his own boyfriend.

"Here's the thing," he said. "If these yahoos wanted Horace dead, couldn't they have killed him today?"

"Yes."

"Wooden swords sound more like movie props to me."

Perry's expression grew animated. "Yes. Exactly. That's it. That's one reason why Horace thinks that this is the work of crazy stalker fans. He believes they tried to use wooden swords because that's what you do with vampires. You drive a wooden stake through their heart. He made a lot of vampire movies."

Okaaay. Judging by the bright eyes and pink cheeks, it was pretty clear that Horace wasn't the only one who thought crazed fans wielding wooden swords made total sense.

"Did Horace report the attack to the police?"

"No. I tried to get him to, but he said he reported the earlier attacks, and nobody believed him. The police thought he was making it up for attention."

Nick grunted. The same thought had occurred to him.

"Even his tenants thought he was imagining things."

"That doesn't seem to be the case." Nick had to allow that much. "You saw these three yourself."

"Yes." Perry's mind was on other things. "In the movie *Why Won't You Die, My Darling?* Horace had to use a giant wooden crucifix to kill Angelina once she became Satan's bride. It's possible someone conflated swords with crucifixes. You see?"

"Mm-hm." Only too well.

"So it does kind of make sense."

Perry went back to watching him with that resolve-weakening mix of confidence and hope. Uneasily, Nick considered the hopefulness. What did Perry want? What were his expectations?

The pork chops were fried to perfection, their fragrant smell warming the small kitchen. Nick slid them from the frying pan onto two thick blue plates, then placed the plates on the table.

"Oh, I'm not hungry," Perry said quickly. Nick guessed that he was thinking—correctly—that two paper-thin pork chops was not a lot of dinner for him. These four beautiful little pork chops would have been a special welcome-home dinner for himself. He had to watch for that kind of thing because Perry was prone to unnecessary self-sacrifice. No way was he going to bed hungry. Not on Nick's watch.

"Did you have dinner?"

"No, but—"

"Eat your dinner."

Perry grimaced, but then smiled as though Nick were offering him a special treat and not his fair share of their rations.

They ate in silence for a few minutes. Nick was tired. It had been a long-ass drive from Modesto. His thoughts were still partly on his case. Perry had had a little adventure, but it was over and no harm done. Nick looked forward to a shower, sleep, and eventually waking up with his favorite person on the entire planet. Rarely did they get a whole weekend to themselves.

Perry chewed a couple of neatly carved pieces of pork before saying slowly, "I really didn't think you'd be home before Monday."

"I wasn't sure I'd be able to get away. Why? Did you make plans?" Nick smiled, a little amused. He took it for granted that if Perry had made plans, he'd change them to accommodate him. Not that he wouldn't fall in with Perry's plans if Perry had his heart set on another art show or something.

Perry looked troubled. "I did, yeah."

Nick's brows rose.

"I told Horace I'd stay up there this weekend."

"You…"

"He needs help, Nick."

"It sounds like it, all right." Nick was unmoved.

Perry seemed to evaluate Nick's mood. He brightened. "What if you stayed up there with me? That would be even better. You know what you're doing."

"What I'm…" Nick swallowed the rest of it. He said very mildly, "Why would you agree to that? Why would you agree to spend the weekend at a falling-down hotel where people in costumes are running around swinging swords at innocent bystanders?"

"I've told you. Horace is afraid," Perry said. "Nobody else believes him."

Nick had no answer for that. Or rather, he had so many answers, he didn't know where to start. He finally managed, "But they'll believe him now. Right? He's got corroborating testimony."

Perry grinned. "'Corroborating testimony.' You're starting to sound like a PI."

"Yeah. But I'm serious. I don't see how it would be of any help to Horace for you to stay over in that dump. What are you supposed to do?"

"I think he's lonely and it's a relief that someone believes him."

"Okay, that's great. But again, what are *you* supposed to do about whatever's going on there?" Nick was struggling not to let his impatience show. Anyway, he was not impatient with Perry. He was impatient with Horace Daly for dragging Perry into his problems.

"Lend moral support?"

"Isn't that nice," Nick said grimly. "But you've had to use your inhaler tonight for the first time in how long? That's not a healthy place for you. Clearly."

Perry colored. His jaw took on that stubborn jut that Nick had become all too familiar with during the past ten months. "I can't not go places just because I have asthma."

"Of course you can. Can't." Nick drew a breath. "Of *course* you can avoid situations that make you s—that aren't good for you. That's just common sense."

"I already agreed to help."

"We're going in circles here. Help him *how*? How does your being there help Daly?"

Perry said, and it sounded like he too was trying to control his impatience, "But that's what I'm saying, Nick. If *you* went with me, *you* could look into it for him. You're trained to do this."

"Look into what?"

"Look into whoever is trying to kill Horace. And why."

Perry's stare was unwavering. Almost stern. Meeting it, Nick's heart sank.

Clearly, he was not going to win this battle. Either he went with Perry or Perry went on his own, but go Perry would. The weekend Nick had in mind was already a write-off.

He struggled for a moment with his disappointment and irritation. Obviously, he could not leave Perry to deal with this bizarre situation on his own. Even if he could, well, there was something about the way Perry looked at him—like he really believed there was nothing Nick couldn't handle, no problem he couldn't solve—and Nick didn't want Perry to ever stop looking at him like that.

Anyway, the main thing was that they had the weekend together. Semper Gumby, right?

"Sounds like you have your mind already made up," Nick said.

His tone was a little flat, and some of the eagerness died out of Perry's face. "You don't want to go?"

"*Want* to go? No. If I do give up my weekend, what do I get out of it?" Nick asked.

Perry continued to eye him in that grave way. "Horace's undying gratitude?" he suggested finally.

"Uh…"

Perry grinned slowly with that funny mixture of sweetness and mischievousness that always set Nick's heart thudding in his chest. "Let me show you."

"I like that," Perry murmured as Nick trailed tiny kisses along his jawline. His lashes were down, and he looked a bit like an angel at rest himself.

Nick grinned at the idea. A wicked angel maybe. "I know you do." Perry loved sex as much as Nick.

That was not a big surprise. The surprise was how adventurous he was. Initially Nick had been very careful to keep everything as vanilla as possible. Knowing how inexperienced and idealistic Perry was, he'd been afraid of shocking him, or even accidentally hurting him. He was such a fragile kid in so many ways.

But he had quickly learned that Perry was, quite literally, up for anything.

That adventurous spirit was one of the many things Nick liked about him. The other thing he really liked—maybe what he liked best—was that Perry was maybe the first genuinely happy person he'd ever known. Not in a simpleminded, too-dumb-to-know-better way. Perry had his moods like everyone else. He got his fair share of hurts and disappointments, but he was by nature optimistic and open. He expected good things but wasn't crushed by setbacks. In his own funny way, he was as tough-minded as any Navy SEAL Nick had known.

Though sex had always been a necessity for Nick, it had not always been happy or joyous. Perry had changed intercourse from pleasurable exercise and much-needed release to something that went way beyond the physical. Nick was not one for greeting-card sentiments, but yeah, being with Perry had taught him the difference between fucking and making love.

Nick kissed Perry's neck, nuzzling delicate collarbones, trailing a path down his sternum, feeling the hard, excited beat of Perry's heart against his lips. In passing, he teasingly flicked the swollen, rosy nubs with his tongue, and Perry arched up with a whimper.

"Like that?"

"Yes," Perry gasped.

Nick continued to nuzzle and nibble his way across the smooth, hairless planes of Perry's chest, trailing down the silky, narrow line of fawn-colored hair that connected belly button to groin.

"I missed you," he muttered.

"Me too. I missed you too. All the time." Perry's wry smile made his face look unexpectedly older.

"It won't always be like this. So much time apart."

"Yeah. But it'll be like this for a while."

That was true. Nick couldn't deny it.

He slid his hand lower to cup Perry's balls, and Perry relaxed his legs, letting them fall open, allowing him better access. Nick shifted so that he could kiss the tip of Perry's swollen cock, licking the bead of precome out of the dark slit with a slow swipe of his tongue.

Perry gulped and stiffened, encouraging Nick with soft, inarticulate sounds.

"Even better than pork chops," Nick told him, and Perry laughed.

But the laughter cracked, turned into wild little cries as Nick's mouth closed on Perry's cock and he began to suck.

"Oh, God. Nick. *Nick*..."

That naked, helpless abandon was a total turn-on—as if Nick needed to be any more turned on. He smiled to himself, working the pale, smooth crown of Perry's penis, licking the underside with the firm tip of his tongue and swirling the rough, broad flat of it over the sensitive tip. Beneath these attentions Perry was almost sobbing, tense, strung tight, eyelashes fluttering, muscles quivering...ready to blow any second.

Zero to sixty, and no apologies needed.

"I love you, Nick. I love you."

The words that half strangled Nick, Perry said easily, almost eagerly, while his narrow hips shoved up, pushing his cock deeper down Nick's throat. Nick loved hearing the words, and he loved that instinctive masculine aggression.

He worked the shaft of Perry's cock, sucking hard, taking long, deep draws, tantalizing, and yeah, maybe tormenting him a little too, pushing Perry to fierce and rapid climax.

Perry's hands clenched in Nick's hair, his back bowed, hips rocking frantically. "*Nick...*" He began to come in hot, white spurts.

Nick swallowed the pulses of his intense, explosive orgasm, before rising to join his mouth to Perry's.

Perry's kisses were sweet and urgent, and Nick returned them deeply, passionately. Once upon a time, kisses—when they happened at all—had been mostly ritual and routine. Now they were an end in themselves, a pleasant way to spend a few minutes, a few hours, even an evening.

Tomorrow would take care of itself. Tonight there was only the two of them...

CHAPTER THREE

A woman kitted out in khaki jodhpurs and a black riding jacket met them as they hiked up the drive to Angel's Rest on Saturday morning.

The barrier at the bottom of the road meant Nick had to park along the busy highway, which he was not happy about. He didn't say he was *un*happy, but it was obvious to Perry.

Clearly Nick felt this entire mission—*mission* being Nick's word, not his—was a waste of time and energy. Nick wanted, and deserved, a nice, relaxing weekend together. Perry wanted that too. Maybe even more than Nick, given that Perry was the one left home and alone much of the time. He'd never say that to Nick, because he knew Nick already worried about him.

Anyway, it was soon clear why the drive had been blocked off. At some point a landslide had occurred, sending boulders and debris tumbling down the dry hillside to land in the road. There were a couple of "potholes" large enough to lose a car the size of Perry's. One of the largest boulders had not continued on its path of destruction. It had touched down mid-center on the driveway, effectively blocking vehicles from both sides.

"Why the hell would Daly not have that rock hauled out of there?" Nick said as the piece of displaced mountain came into view.

"Maybe he can't afford to. I don't think he's got much money." Or maybe Horace liked his privacy. Or both.

It was right about then the lady in riding clothes appeared, casually strolling along the moonscape of driveway.

Spotting Perry and Nick, she raised her riding crop—yep, that was a riding crop—and called, "Is my taxi waiting?"

Perry and Nick glanced at each other.

"No taxi that I saw, ma'am," Nick answered.

She frowned. "Damn. If this keeps up, I'm going to start using another company."

As they drew even with her, Perry could see that she was not nearly as young as he'd assumed given her jet-black hair and trim figure. She could have been anywhere from late sixties to early eighties.

She nodded politely and strode briskly past, the heels of her riding boots crunching on the sandy pavement.

"Maybe her horse threw her," Perry replied to what he knew Nick was thinking.

"Out of the movie?" Nick muttered.

Perry chuckled. "I'm sure she lives at the hotel. There's no place else around here."

"Great. You're doing nothing to relieve my concerns."

Perry chuckled again.

They rounded the boulder—which was about the size of a small garden shed—and continued up the tree-lined drive.

"She's not one of the ones I met yesterday." Perry was thinking. "There was a guy about your age called Ned Duke. I think he's a screenwriter. Or wants to be a screenwriter. And then there was a lady with purple-and-green hair named Gilda Storm. She's a psychic." He watched Nick as he said it because he knew Nick had zero patience with the idea of psychics. Sure enough, Nick made a pained sound.

"There's Ami. Horace said she works for the studio, but he didn't say doing what and he didn't say which studio. And there was Enzo Juri. He used to be Horace's driver and bodyguard."

"Judging by the state of this road, it doesn't look like Daly has a lot of use for a driver."

"True."

"Where was Juri when the skeleton crew jumped his boss?"

"Well, I don't think he's still working as a bodyguard," Perry said. "I think he's just another tenant now."

"How many tenants altogether did you say?"

"Seven."

Nick made no comment, maybe because the hotel was now in view. All eight stories. Angel's Rest was a 1920s architectural gem of tall windows and fancy cornices, finials and gargoyles, steep slanting roofs and round stone towers.

It looked even grander from the front than it had from the back, and Perry wondered if he could maybe squeeze a little sketching time into the afternoon.

Nick came to a stop, hands on hips, studying the building as though considering how best to rig it to detonate.

"Asbestos shingles, I'll guaran-damn-tee it."

Perry snorted.

"It's no joke."

"No, I know. It's just...you have to admit it's kind of amazing."

"It's amazing all right," Nick said in a tone that equated *amazing* with *death trap*. He gave Perry a sideways look, and meeting Perry's gaze, shook his head. "You'll be lucky if the hot water works."

"The hot water works. I washed up in Horace's bathroom yesterday."

Nick sighed.

"It's another adventure." Perry patted Nick's back in encouragement.

It was Nick's turn to laugh.

A portly man in baggy red corduroy pants and a black and white checked flannel shirt greeted them at the front entrance, opening the tall carved door before they could ring the bell.

He was about sixty, with thinning gray hair and whiskery jowls. Though Perry had not met him the day before, the man seemed to be expecting them. Or at least, expecting Perry. He seemed taken aback by Nick's presence but recovered quickly.

"Hi," Perry began. "I'm—"

"Oh, I know who you are," the man interrupted in a nervous, hushed voice. "And right on time, aren't you?"

Well, yes, they were, so there wasn't much to say in response, even if they'd been allowed to answer, which they were not.

"I need to talk to you, son," the man said to Perry. "Before you speak to Horace again."

Something about him put Perry's back up. Maybe it was the furtive way he glanced around the hall as though he knew he was doing something he shouldn't. Maybe it was the way he had instantly dismissed Nick. Or maybe it was the smell of beer on his breath. Not that Perry objected to beer drinking, but beer drinking at ten in the morning?

"And you are?" Nick asked.

The man threw him a harassed look before pinning his watery gaze on Perry again. "Jonah Nevin. I'm Horace's cousin by marriage. Sissy is his only living relation. I don't mean to make a mystery of things. You'll understand once you've spoken to Sissy."

"Okay," Perry said doubtfully, not liking this at all. He liked it less as Jonah scuttled down the hall ahead of them, as though afraid of being intercepted.

Judging by the austere line of Nick's profile, he wasn't crazy about the situation either. Nick always preferred a straightforward approach, and this—without hearing a word from Cousin Sissy—already felt like they were going behind Horace's back.

Perry had a quick impression of a huge gray marble foyer with tall columns, stylized light fixtures, and a ceiling painted in a vibrant gold, red, and blue art deco design. The lighting was bad, but not so bad that he couldn't see the moth-eaten state of carpets, drapes, and upholstery on the remaining pieces of furniture. The evening before he'd been too distracted to take much heed of his surroundings—beyond noting the occasional ghostly or cadaverous figure positioned for best effect in the gloom.

"Right this way," Jonah threw back, still scurrying along.

He led them up a short marble staircase, down a hall, finally coming to a stop at a half-open door. He rapped on the door and pushed it wide.

"Here we are, Mother!" he announced.

A large woman in a blue-print muumuu rose from the sofa. "Oh, goody! Bring him through, Father."

She was tall—taller than himself or even Nick—and big-boned, but she was also very obese. Her faded golden hair was shoulder-length and styled in a sixties' flip. Her lipstick was pink, her eye shadow turquoise, but her features seemed blurred and indistinct.

"Oh, my word. There's two of them!" she exclaimed, looking from Perry to Nick.

"This is Nick Reno," Perry said. "I'm Perry Foster."

"It's a pleasure to meet you, Perry. Nick. I'm Sissy Nevin. Thank you for agreeing to speak to me." She gave a breathy, girlish laugh. "I guess this seems pretty strange, but it's a strange situation."

"No argument here," Nick said.

Sissy gave another of those breathy laughs. "Now sit down, boys! Would you like something to drink? Father, get our guests something cool to drink. I guess you've had a walk. It's hot out there. Hot for October."

Jonah disappeared through a tall swinging door into what was probably the kitchen. Sissy kept talking and making little *sit-down* gestures, so Perry obediently folded onto a squat, green love seat. The plump cushions seemed to compress, and he felt himself sinking.

Nick's expression was a study, and Perry had to gulp back an inappropriate gurgle of laughter. It was like they'd fallen down a rabbit hole or maybe through the *Looking Glass*. The whole visit was taking on a Wonderland feel.

Nick bypassed the man-eating love seat and selected a sturdy little hardback chair next to an old-fashioned sewing machine table, which was stationed at the window overlooking the green swamp of the nearly empty swimming pool.

"Now, I hope you won't take offense if I speak freely," Sissy was saying. "I'm Horace's only living relative, and it's only natural I'd be concerned for him."

"Sure," Perry said politely.

"I can see you're nice boys, and I know you want to help." She threw back her head and yelled, "Father, there's pink lemonade already made in the icebox!"

Perry risked another glance at Nick. Nick gave him a level look, and Perry hastily looked away.

Sissy beamed at them. "Horace has always been...well, different. You must have noticed that yourself. But he's perfectly harmless. That other time wasn't really his fault. Troy brought that on himself. I'm not judging. It's a fact."

"What is it you're not judging?" Nick asked.

Perry asked at the same time, "What's a fact?"

Sissy answered Nick. "Horace was raised in a good Christian home. His choices are his own. I'm not judging."

Perry suddenly realized where this was headed—he had briefly wondered about Horace—and he tried to lift out of the smooshy love-seat cushions, but he was sitting at a weird angle and couldn't quite get leverage.

Jonah shoved out past the kitchen's swinging door, precariously balancing a tray with a pitcher of pink liquid and four glasses. He said heartily, "Who wants lemonade?"

"We all want lemonade, Father," Sissy said, and without missing a beat, returned to her previous train of thought. "When Horace stabbed Troy, they were both doing drugs. That was the culture back then, wasn't it? He's never been violent since. The hallucinations are something else, and that might be from taking all those pills for so long. I don't know, and the doctors couldn't really say."

Her pink mouth smiled at Perry, and she blinked her blue eyelids a couple of times. He automatically took the glass of lemonade Jonah handed him.

"What happened yesterday wasn't a hallucination," Perry said.

All at once the room seemed very quiet.

"Of course, if you say so, I would have to believe you," Sissy said finally.

Now he could see her eyes were very small and very dark. Like raisins in dough.

"I do say so."

She gave that gusty little laugh. "So you do! But you know, there was never anyone there those other times. Father looked and looked. Didn't you, Father?"

"Yes," Jonah said grimly. "I surely did."

"And Mr. Juri and Mr. Duke looked as well."

"There were three of them yesterday," Perry said. "Three assailants. They wore costumes and carried wooden swords."

Sissy licked her lips and reached for her lemonade. She drank half the glass in a single gulp. The cold beverage seemed to fortify her. "They could have run away those other times," she agreed.

"They don't know the whole story, Mother," Jonah said.

"Why don't you tell us the whole story?" Nick asked. "Since that's the reason you brought us up here."

Sissy gave him that pink Cheshire Cat smile again. "I like you, Nick. You're a forthright young man. The truth is, poor cousin Horace has been claiming people are trying to kill him for years. The only one who ever did really try was poor Troy, and that was in self-defense, to my way of thinking. It's been a long time since Horace saw any ghosts and such, and I thought we were past all that."

Jonah said flatly, "He had to be locked up the last time. They put him in the loony bin. That's what we're afraid of. We don't want you to encourage him."

Perry set his glass on the floor. He rocked forward hard, and this time managed to eject himself from the love seat. He could see out of the corner of his eye that Nick had also risen.

"I don't know anything about Mr. Daly's past, but he didn't make up a story about being attacked yesterday," Perry said. "I saw his attackers. I fought with one of them. He was just as real as either of you."

"Now please don't be offended," Sissy said. She was still smiling up at them. "Sometimes Horace makes friends with young men, but those friendships usually don't last once they realize he hasn't any money. Not anymore. It's all long gone. Mostly spent on booze and drugs, sad to say."

"I see. Thank you for your honesty," Perry said. His face felt hot. His heart was beating fast with anger and outrage. What exactly was this awful woman accusing them of? He wasn't even sure.

"Honesty is the best policy," Sissy assured them.

Jonah saw them to the door. "You can't say you weren't warned," he remarked. His tone was conversational rather than confrontational, which really just made it all the creepier.

"No, we couldn't say that," Perry replied.

Jonah nodded curtly and closed the door in their faces.

"Jesus Christ," Nick said quietly as they headed back to the marble lobby.

"If anybody's crazy, it's them," Perry said. He was surprised when Nick rested his hand briefly on his shoulder.

Perry's sympathy was entirely with Horace, but at the same time he was uncomfortably aware that the situation at Angel's Rest was not what he'd imagined, and he'd dragged Nick right into the middle of it. Maybe he should be comforting Nick.

They retraced their steps to the lobby, where they found Enzo Juri—Horace's former bodyguard and driver—waiting for them.

Perry had met Enzo the evening before when Horace had invited him to wash up in his rooms, but he hadn't really formed much of an opinion. There were so many oddballs in the house, it was difficult to judge people as you would if you'd met them in the outside world.

But maybe Enzo wasn't waiting for them. Maybe he was just there. He held a small parcel wrapped in what appeared to be white butcher's paper, and he reminded Perry of someone waiting for a bus that had changed routes. He looked surprised when they strolled down the steps leading into the foyer.

"You're back!" he said to Perry.

"Mr. Daly asked me to come back," Perry said. He thought Juri had been present when Horace had issued his invitation, but in all honesty, the evening—except for the parts spent with Nick—was starting to run together. Maybe Enzo had left by then.

"Sure. That's right." Enzo's smile was vague. He tossed the white parcel from hand to hand, like an absentminded pitcher. "I didn't think you would, though."

Under the scars and weathering, he was probably about Horace's age. They appeared to have been a rough seventy-plus years, but then according to Horace, Enzo had been a professional boxer and a bouncer as well as a bodyguard. He looked like a former boxer: medium height and solid as a rock, even given his age. He had a blunt-featured, lumpy face with mild, vaguely mournful dark eyes.

"Why wouldn't I come back?" Perry asked. "I said I would."

Enzo scratched his head. His hair, what there was of it, was white and buzz-cut very close to his scalp. "It's just…why would you want to get mixed up in this?"

"In what?" Nick asked.

"Our happy home," Enzo said with unexpected irony.

Before either of them could respond, he added, "Sissy got to you, I guess?"

"She wanted to talk to us before we saw Mr. Daly," Perry said.

Enzo laughed. "I bet she did. Well, maybe it's all true. So what? You ask me, I think the place *is* haunted."

Nick's silence was as loud as thunder.

Perry did not believe in ghosts. Living at the old Alston Estate had given him ample proof that however scary and supernatural events might seem, there was always human agency behind them.

He asked, "Haunted by who?"

A furtive look seemed to flicker in Enzo's dark eyes. "Take your pick. Plenty of people have died in this wreck."

Nick said, "Like?"

"You ever heard of Rudolph Dennings?"

"Nope."

"He was a big name in the twenties. Westerns. You know the kind of thing. Rope tricks and quick draw. He had a trained cowpony named Belle he used to keep out in the stables between pictures. Well, when the talkies came in, it turned out that Dennings had one of those snooty English accents, and every time he opened his mouth on screen, audiences burst out laughing. He couldn't get work. So one night, he jumped out of his window on the eighth floor. People say they see his ghost falling past their windows."

Perry opened his mouth, but Enzo wasn't done. "June Kent was another one. She wasn't an actress, though. She was a rich socialite in love with Wendell Warren, who you're also probably too young to have ever heard of. Kent left her husband for Warren, but then Warren changed his mind, and Kent shot herself beside the swimming pool."

"That's terrible," Perry said. He felt the look Nick threw him, but he was thinking more of the desperately unhappy girl who'd killed herself rather than the desperately unhappy ghost possibly haunting the premises. Perry knew how it felt to get your heart broken. Or at least how it felt when you *thought* your heart was broken.

Enzo said, "It sure is. Once a place gets a reputation for being haunted, you play hell trying to sell it. Even if the real-estate market hadn't gone kablooey." He shrugged. "Dennings and Kent. Those were the two who put us out of business. A bunch of dopers and down-and-outers ODed here during the sixties and seventies, but their ghosts would be too addled to find their way out of their coffins."

Wow. And here Perry had thought the conversation with Cousin Sissy and Uncle Jonah was peculiar?

Nick made a sound too pained for a sigh and too quiet for a groan.

Perry said, "I didn't see a ghost, though. I saw three people in skeleton costumes and capes. Just as real as the three of us standing here."

Enzo studied him skeptically. "Tell you the truth, I think it would be better if you claimed you'd seen a ghost."

"How do you figure that?" Nick asked.

"I'd rather deal with ghosts than one of those LA gangs."

"A *gang*?" Perry repeated.

"What else? Early trick-or-treaters?"

Good question. The state of the back gardens indicated people were using the hotel grounds for less than savory pastimes, maybe even illegal activities, but the idea of gangs—let alone gangs in capes—prowling Laurel Canyon seemed pretty far-fetched.

"I don't know of any gangs that dress up in fancy costumes and carry wooden swords," Nick said, following Perry's line of thought. "Usually they go for baggy pants, baseball caps worn backward, and semiautomatic pistols."

Enzo opened his mouth, but before he could speak, a woman began to scream from down the hall.

CHAPTER FOUR

Nick was expecting...oh hell, maybe another appearance by the Over-The-Hill-And-Then-Some gang? He wasn't sure. He didn't fail to note that by the second scream, there was a note of outrage amid all the blood-curdling. Working at catching cheating spouses mid-act had given him great familiarity with outraged females, and he was familiar with that particular decibel.

So as he skidded around the corner—despite the lack of regular mopping, the marble floors were more slippery than glass—he was not anticipating having to pull his weapon. Until he saw the alligator.

Yeah. A thirteen-foot alligator was trying to cram through the scratched and battered door to one of the apartments. The woman struggling to get the door shut was still screaming, but there were words now—plenty of them.

"Goddamn it, Enzo! Wally's inside again!" the woman shrieked. "Enzo? Anybody? Can anybody hear me?"

Yes, people heard her. And if they missed her screams, they could hardly miss the ungodly noise the gator was making—a rumbling roar that sounded more big cat than reptilian. The smell was revolting. A musky blend of mud and dead and decaying fish.

A door at the opposite end of the hall flew open, and a woman with a green and purple bush on her head—that couldn't be hair, could it?—stuck her head out and then immediately slammed shut her door again. Gee, it was almost like old times at the Alston Estate.

The door opposite the bush lady flew open, and a guy around Nick's age burst out and stumbled toward the alligator, adding his yells to the general pandemonium. "Enzo! Enzo! The fucking lizard's out again. In again. The alligator's inside!"

Nick slid to a stop, raising his weapon.

"No! No! Christ, don't shoot it! *Don't shoot!*" That was Juri, who had followed Nick and Perry from the foyer.

Perry panted, "Nick, don't shoot. It's a pet."

"A *pet*?" Nick threw him a quick, disbelieving look.

Perry nodded quickly.

Juri was still pleading. "Don't shoot Wally. Please. He's not dangerous."

"The hell he's not dangerous," yelled the younger man from down the hall. He had blue-black eyes, long dark hair, and one of those unfortunate beards that were supposed to look cool—assuming your idea of style was Moses or elderly hillbillies.

"Look, look!" Juri hastily unwrapped the small white parcel that turned out to contain glistening red chunks of liver and other offal. The wrapper floated to the marble floor as he waved a fistful of meat frantically. "Wally! Wally! Look here, boy! Come here!"

At the sound of Juri's voice, the alligator raised its long, ugly head and appeared to sniff the air. Its massive tail swept back and forth as it began to reverse. Nick and everyone else in the hall jumped out of range.

"There. You see?" Juri exclaimed. "He's leaving. He just got confused. He didn't mean any harm. It's my fault for leaving the gate open."

"Then maybe he should shoot you," Long Hair retorted. "My ass, he's harmless! If he'd got through that door—"

The door in question opened cautiously. A young woman with curly brown hair and wide green eyes craned her head around the edge. "You *promised*, Enzo," she said. "You said it would never happen again."

"I know, I know. I could have sworn I shut the gate." Juri was walking backward, still waving the meat. "I don't know what went wrong."

"I'll tell you what went wrong," Long Hair said. "You forgot to lock the goddamned gate."

Juri had reached one of the tall, arched glass doors. He fumbled with the latch, shoved it open, and stepped outside, still making clucking sounds and calling to the alligator, who slowly followed him.

"Jesus fucking Christ." The guy with the long hair looked at the girl. "Are you okay, Ami?"

She nodded, looked at Nick, looked at the pistol. "Thank you. I thought he was really coming through the door that time."

"It's happened before?" Nick asked. He holstered his weapon.

"Last month. He's a pet, but still."

The young man said, "And two months before that, he got out. You can't domesticate wild animals. Imagine if one of us stepped out of our room at night and that thing was running loose in the dark. It belongs in a zoo."

"I know." The girl shuddered. "But he's had him for forty years."

"Hell, put Juri in the zoo with him."

"What's going on here? What's happened?" The voice was somehow familiar, although it had probably been twenty years since the last time Nick had seen a Horace Daly movie.

They all turned to face the newcomer.

Yep, Horace Daly, in the flesh. He was tall, slender, and unexpectedly elegant despite the scuffed tennis shoes, worn jeans, and wrinkled white denim shirt. His hair was long and silver, and even from all the way down the hall Nick could see how blue his eyes were.

Long Hair and the girl both started talking at once.

"Wally tried to get into my apartment again," Ami said. "He nearly took the door down this time."

"That thing's a menace. Something's got to be done," the man—presumably Ned Duke—insisted.

"Have you spoken to Enzo?" Horace's crystal gaze fell on Perry. "My dear boy! You came! You kept your promise!"

"Yes, I—"

"I *knew* you were a man of principle. The moment I laid eyes on you."

"Oh. Thank you, but—"

"But where are your bags?"

"In the car," Perry said. "We had to park down by the road."

Horace was beaming at Perry, but then the "we" registered, and he belatedly noticed Nick. His expression seemed to change to one of wariness before smoothing out to a courteous blank. He offered his hand. "I'm sorry. I don't believe we've met."

Nick shook hands. Horace's skin was cold and dry, but there was plenty of strength in his grip.

Duke, meanwhile, wasn't giving up. "What happens if that monster gets through the door next time, Horace?"

Horace ignored him. Pointedly.

Perry said, "This is Nick Reno. I told you about him yesterday."

Horace smiled, but his eyes did not warm. "Ah, yes. The PI. But I thought you were out of town?"

"Nick got back last night."

"It's illegal to keep an alligator as a pet in Los Angeles county," Duke persisted. "I looked it up. Maybe somebody needs to call Animal Control."

Horace stopped smiling and turned back to Duke. "Not if that somebody intends to keep living at Angel's Rest."

The girl murmured in dismay.

Duke's face tightened. "I'm not sure low rent is worth the risk of being eaten by an alligator."

"*Eaten* by an alligator?" Horace made a dismissive noise. "No one has been eaten in four decades. I think you're safe enough. Ami, lovey, were you harmed in any way?"

"Well, no. But…"

"It would break Enzo's heart if something happened to Wally. Do you want to break Enzo's heart?"

Ami glanced at Duke and sighed. "No. But I also d—"

"Excellent," Horace said with finality. "Then we're all in agreement." He turned to Perry and switched the smile back on. "I'm ecstatic you came. Let's go where we can speak in private."

Perry offered Nick a look that was half apology and half *now-the-adventure-begins!* and followed Horace, who strode swiftly down the long, gloomy corridor. Nick walked behind them, observing and assessing. Through the grimy arched windows, he could see Enzo still coaxing the alligator across the patchy lawn toward an opening in the hedge. That was one very big lizard, and Nick's sympathies were all with Ami and Duke.

"Arrogant little shit. I don't appreciate being threatened," Horace was muttering as he opened the ornate bronze gate to a small elevator at the end of the hall. "It's hard to find good tenants, though, and the Duke boy has never missed a rent check yet."

The three of them crowded into the ornamental-looking elevator, Horace slid the gate shut with a *clang*, pressed a button, and the small cage lifted slowly and, it seemed to Nick, none-too-steadily from the hall. The pulleys squeaked ominously as the floors inched past. Horace talked all the while—and, in Nick's opinion, to no purpose. Just filling the silence? There was a lot to fill in a place this big.

The lift lurched to a stop on the third level, and Horace shoved back the gate and gestured for them to disembark. "I'm the only one on this floor. The rest of them are downstairs. I like my privacy."

He led the way down another much darker hallway, past a mannequin in a monk's robe and hood. Most of the lighting provided by the retrofitted wall sconces was flickering or non-existent. Still, from what he could tell, the scarlet and gold carpet was in better shape up here and the watered silk wallpaper mostly intact. A skull with a knife through the eye sat on a tall, narrow library table, but what caught Nick's attention—and that was likely due to nearly a year of living with Perry—was the artwork. A gallery of large, framed paintings in a variety of mostly disturbing styles stretched all the way from the elevator to as far down the hall as he could see.

Nick spent a lot of time in motels and hotels, and it was safe to say this art was very different from the generic photographs of lighthouses and floral watercolors that graced most of his lodgings.

"Pretty cool, right?" Perry said, watching his reaction. "These are all paintings from Mr. Daly's films."

"Is that so?" Nick had guessed as much. He couldn't imagine there was a big demand for landscapes featuring gallows trees and graveyards outside of the movie industry.

"I always made sure to make friends with my film set decorators," Horace put in. "Of course, none of this is worth anything to anyone but me."

"There's some good stuff here." Perry assured Nick, as though reading his mind.

"Yeah?"

"Yeah. Well, I don't mean valuable necessarily, but that's a great try at cubism, and it's an actual painting, not a print." Perry nodded at what looked like a portrait of a woman hacked to pieces. Eye of the beholder stuff, for sure.

Perry and Horace chattered on about the prop paintings until they reached Horace's room. Horace unlocked the door and ushered them inside rooms that smelled of must, mothballs, and marijuana.

Wow, in Perry's words.

Horace's quarters were actually a couple of presidential-sized suites with the dividing wall knocked down in order to create one large and luxurious apartment. Or at least at one time it would have been luxurious. Now... The first thing Nick noticed was the enormous picture window overlooking the dead garden. The window let in a lot of daylight which, after the disturbing hallway art gallery, was welcome. The second thing he noticed was that the place looked more like a film set than a place where anyone actually lived.

A huge gold and black mummy case stood propped against one wall. At the dining table across the room, a skeleton in a cape and top hat was seated opposite a second skeleton wearing a tuxedo and a horse skull for a head.

"Homey, isn't it?" Nick said, and Perry grinned at him.

"I like to have my toys about me," Horace said. He was preening. Did he imagine most people would be anything but creeped out by this collection of macabre memorabilia? Or maybe he liked the idea of creeping people out?

"I see that."

There were toys in the room, as a matter of fact. A heavy bookcase was crowded with old-fashioned tops and jack-in-the-boxes and tin soldiers—probably worth a pretty penny on eBay—and on the top shelf, a row of creepy, antique dolls in frilly dresses slumped against each other.

Having visited this personal museum the day before, Perry's attention was focused on Horace. He was saying, "I told Nick all about your situation. I think he can help you."

Horace doubtfully surveyed Nick. "Let's talk in the kitchen where we can't be overheard," he said.

Overheard by what? The skeletons? The dolls with their bright, empty eyes? Whatever was residing in that mummy case?

But Nick said nothing, following Horace and Perry through the open doorway into the adjoining room. Here at least the smells were more ordinary: burned bacon and a drain that could have used a box or two of baking soda. A bottle of sage-and-lavender-scented cleaning solution sat on the metal-edged linoleum counter.

Horace went straight to the kitchen sink and turned the taps on full. He beckoned to Nick and Perry to join him.

As they edged close, he put his finger to his lips. Nick gave Perry a side look, but Perry was watching Horace attentively.

When Horace decided the rush of water had reached the right decibel, he spoke in a low but carrying voice. "I can't tell you how grateful I am that you kept your word."

"Of course," Perry said. Serious and solemn. Concerned for Horace. Indifferent to the weirdness of the situation. Nick shook his head inwardly and let his impatience go. Perry had committed to this plan of action, therefore Nick was committed. That was how it was.

"All I need is someone to stay here until Monday morning. Once Halloween is past, the danger will be over."

Nick said, "I'm not following."

"Just having someone here during the...the critical period will act as a deterrent. I truly don't believe he—*they* will try anything now."

Horace gazed at them with blazing-eyed earnestness that did nothing to reassure Nick.

"You don't believe who will try what?" Nick asked. He hadn't missed the *he* being belatedly switched out for *they*.

Horace pointed silently, meaningfully at the floor.

Meaning friends, family, or tenants? All of the above? None of the above?

Nick could not say what he was thinking—not with Perry gazing at him with that mix of hope and confidence. Hope that this would make sense to Nick. Confidence that once it did, Nick would have a ready solution.

"Why would the danger pass with Halloween?"

"Because," Horace said quickly. "*Because.*"

"Yeah, that really doesn't expl—"

"I was thinking about this after we spoke last night." Horace was talking to Perry again, and Perry was nodding encouragingly. "I started remembering. The last time this happened, it was around Halloween as well. I'm almost positive that every time it starts up again, it's around Halloween. Which makes sense."

No. Not really. Not even to Perry, who was now shooting Nick uneasy little glances.

"When what starts up again?" Nick persisted.

"The attempts on my life!"

"I see. You're saying you believe every Halloween someone attempts to kill you?"

"Yes. I don't believe it. I know it. That's when the letters arrive." Horace frowned. "Well, not every Halloween. And this time *is* different. This is the first time assassins were sent after me."

Assassins.

Horace was the original drama queen, but maybe it came with the territory.

"Mr. Daly, is it at all possible that yesterday's attackers were pranking you?"

"*Pranking* me?" Horace's brows rose in offended inquiry.

"Playing a practical joke on you. Maybe someone with a peculiar sense of humor?"

Horace frowned over this idea for a moment or two before admitting grudgingly, "Perhaps. I *might* accept that explanation if there hadn't been three of them."

"I don't see the significance of three attackers."

Perry said, "How realistic is it someone could persuade three people to take part in a potentially fatal practical joke?"

"For the right amount of money? Very. Dumb people do dumb things for money."

"But why would someone pay for that? Besides, those guys weren't professionals, but they also weren't kidding around yesterday."

Fair enough. And Perry was in a position to know how serious Horace's assailants had been, having nearly fallen victim to them as well.

"Okay," Nick said. "Not a bad joke, then. You believe that someone in this house wants you out of the way?"

Despite his earlier hints, Horace hesitated. "It's possible. Or it could be someone obsessed with my films." Horace nodded at Perry, as though that was Perry's theory.

A limitless cast of suspects. Great.

"Perry said you've received threatening letters. Did you keep any of the letters? Did you keep the envelopes?"

"No."

Nick wasn't sure if he was lying or not. The problem with Horace's films had never been Horace's acting.

Nick said, "Do you remember if the letters came in the mail?"

"Yes." Horace frowned, considering. Or pretending to consider? "I think so. I think they came in the mail."

"Do you remember if the stamps on the envelopes were cancelled?"

"I...don't remember. It isn't something I looked for."

That was hard to believe. Who wouldn't at least glance at the envelope after receiving a death threat? Then again, Horace did seem to live in his own little world.

"If these threats aren't coming from a crazed fan, who do you think might wish you harm?"

Once again, Horace hesitated. He said without conviction, "I can't think of anyone."

"Who gains from your death?"

Horace gave a weird laugh. "As of this morning?" He nodded at Perry. "Perry does."

CHAPTER FIVE

"**H**uh?" Perry looked from Nick to Horace, then back to Nick. "Wait. What?"

He'd read about people's faces looking like thunderclouds, but this was the first time he'd actually witnessed it. He could practically see lightning bolts glinting in Nick's eyes.

"What does that mean?" Nick said with ominous restraint.

Horace's smile was a little unsettling. "Last night I phoned my lawyer, he drew up a new will, and I signed it first thing this morning."

"Why would you do that?" Nick asked. It was Perry's question too.

Maybe Nick's displeasure was finally starting to register because Horace seemed a little flustered. "I-I realized yesterday that Perry is a man of extraordinary tal—"

Nick broke in. "I repeat. Why would you do that?"

"After Perry explained his situation last night—"

This was more and more confusing. Never mind the fact that Horace was living like a refugee from the Hollywood Horror Museum. Nick was liable to think…what? That Perry had been complaining about money—or, more exactly, the fact that they didn't have any? He hadn't. Wouldn't. Besides, compared to his previous precarious financial situation, they were living like kings. Well, princes. Princes on a fixed income. It didn't matter. He'd be happy to live in a cardboard box so long as it was with Nick.

"You think someone in this house might have a motive to kill you, and knowing that, you changed your will in favor of *Perry?*"

Perry put his hand on Nick's arm, feeling the rigidity of tendons, the bulge of muscles. Nick was mad enough to punch something. Or someone. "It's okay—"

"No, it's not okay."

Horace was stammering, "Well, *yes*. If anyone here imagined they had a reason to want me out of the way, that reason is gone. I signed it away at 9:15 this morning."

"And turned Perry into a potential target."

Okay. *Now* he got it. Now he understood the underlying cause of Nick's tension. Nick had a tendency to be a little... overprotective. Sometimes. But really, wasn't the most likely explanation of Horace's troubles a crazed fan who couldn't tell the difference between reality and special effects?

Although... If the unpleasant Nevins were hoping to inherit whatever remained of Horace's fortune, this decision of Horace's would not go over well.

"No, no," Horace was saying quickly. "There would be no reason. The will is signed. It's over and done. Now my estate goes to whoever Perry designates."

"What are you—? Are you—? You're not *dead*," Nick snapped. "Perry wouldn't inherit until you're out of the way. If something happens to Perry before you die, it means you'd either have to choose another heir or the estate goes to *your* next of kin."

Accurate and absolute. Like a well-aimed bullet. That was Nick.

Horace looked genuinely confused, so maybe Sissy and Jonah were right about his not being mentally all there. "Anyway, it's just a precaution," he protested. "No one is after me for my money!"

"Then why change your will? What are they after you for?"

"Nick—"

He might as well be talking to himself. Nick continued to ignore him, staring at poor, red-faced and trembling Horace as though drawing a bead on him.

Horace grabbed at the rags of his dignity. "I think you should leave," he announced in a huffy voice.

"I think you're right."

Perry opened his mouth, and Nick added, "And Perry is coming with me."

"*No,*" Horace cried. He turned to Perry. "You promised to help."

"Nick, he needs help. That's why we're here."

Nick's blue gaze was bleak. "That was before we heard the whole story."

Yeah, but they hadn't heard the whole story. That much was obvious. What was also obvious was Horace's fear. That was real. Maybe the most real thing about Horace.

Perry squeezed Nick's arm. "Come on, Nick. We can't just leave it like this." Nick opened his mouth, but Perry hurried on. "Mr. Daly could have been seriously injured yesterday."

Better him than you. Nick didn't say it, but it was right there in his eyes.

It warmed Perry—no one had ever cared about him the way Nick did. Well, his mom and dad, of course, but that was different. At the same time, this was Perry's decision too, right?

Perry answered Nick's silent protest. "Anyway, it's just two nights. And what could happen with you here to protect me?"

He was joking—at least partly joking. Nick scowled. Horace said, "*Yes*, it's only for two nights. Just until Halloween is over. After that everything will go back to normal. I'm sure it will."

He sounded more hopeful than sure.

Reading their expressions, Horace rushed on. "I-I apologize for losing my temper. My nerves aren't good. Of course, you're welcome to stay as well, Mr. Reno."

Nick snorted. Probably at the idea that Horace was doing him a favor by extending the invitation to him. Perry grinned—inviting him to share the joke—and after a moment, Nick said grudgingly, "All right. We'll stay the weekend."

"*Thank you, thank you, thank you!*" Horace cried. He meant it too, but the stagey way he said everything always made him sound like he was delivering lines in a play.

Nick continued grimly, "On condition that you keep the news about changing your will to yourself."

Something sly and secretive seemed to flit through Horace's pale gaze. Then it was gone. He smiled broadly.

"Of course! My dear boy! *Of course*. It shall all be *exactly* as you say."

Ding. Ding. Ding.

"I have an announcement to make!" Horace stood at the head of the mile-long, slightly battered dining table, chiming his dessert spoon against his wineglass.

"Of course you do, darling," Wynne Winthrop said. She was the black-haired woman in jodhpurs Perry and Nick had spoken to that morning on their way to Angel's Rest. According to Horace, Wynne was a long-time friend and frequent costar. Maybe props and set decorations weren't the only things Horace collected from his days in the movies.

It was Saturday night, about eight hours after Perry and Nick's arrival at the hotel, and Perry was increasingly sure he had made a huge mistake coercing Nick into spending one of his rare weekends at Angel's Rest.

For someone who believed his life was in danger, Horace had been strangely disinterested in talking to Nick about who or what might wish him harm. Even Perry, who was not suspicious by nature, couldn't help but believe Horace knew a lot more than he was letting on. He also couldn't help wondering if what Horace secretly wanted was really just…company. Because they'd spent the entire day listening to him relive his career in the movie industry. Maybe Horace was frightened, but he was even more lonely.

So that was the first thing. The second thing was Perry was not feeling great. The dust and general decay of the building were bothering him more than he'd expected—or was willing to admit to Nick. If there were not mold spores floating around with all the pollen and dander, it would be a miracle. After months of rarely having to resort to using his inhaler, it was demoralizing to feel so wheezy and breathless again.

Anyway, now they were seated with the rest of the building's tenants in the once grand formal dining hall. Ami Savitri had prepared dinner for the entire household, which, according to Horace, was a weekly event. Ami got reduced rent for her efforts, and the residents who chose to partake of the meal paid her a nominal fee. It seemed to Perry that this was another way for Horace to guarantee he had company at least once a week, although it was unclear whether Horace actually liked his tenants or not.

The good news was the food looked good and smelled better. The pungent aroma of garlic, basil, oregano, and rosemary warmed the air as lasagna, spaghetti bolognese, pasta primavera, green salad, and long loaves of buttery garlic bread were placed on the long table. Plenty of food for people who tucked in like it was their first and only meal of the week. Maybe it was. It seemed pretty clear that no one at Angel's Rest was living high on the hog, including Horace.

Judging by the anticipation on everyone's faces as they began to pass the casserole dishes and bowls around the table, it was going to be a very good dinner. Or would have been. Perry was afraid Horace's announcement was about to ruin—at the very least—Nick's appetite.

Nick already looked—once again—like a volcano about to blow.

"Goddamn it," he said softly. "I knew it."

Perry was not completely surprised either, assuming what they feared was coming actually transpired. Hearing Horace reminiscence about his drug-fueled days in the movie industry had not inspired a lot of confidence in their host's promises. Not that Horace wasn't sober and aware of what he was doing. He'd filled his wineglass with mineral water, so that alarming glitter in his eyes was not due to artificial stimulants.

Cousin Sissy, watching Cousin Jonah serve her a slab of lasagna, said, "Maybe you could save your announcement for after we enjoy this meal we've paid for in peace."

Enzo glared across the table at her, but Sissy's attention remained elsewhere. She pointed at the platter of spaghetti traveling their way. Jonah waggled the serving spoon he'd taken from the lasagna dish in readiness.

"What are we toasting to?" Gilda, the purple-haired psychic, inquired, raising her wineglass.

Horace frowned. "We're not toasting. This is not cause for celebration."

"No? Oh." Gilda smiled vaguely. "In that case." She tossed back her wine in a single gulp.

The wind had picked up that afternoon—California's weather was predictably unpredictable—and a draft whispered through the cracked casements of the Palladian windows and tickled the back of Perry's neck. He shivered. Nick threw him a quick, concerned look. Perry grimaced.

Horace, ignoring the antics of those in the cheaper seats, continued in a lofty tone. "Since no one here chooses to believe that my life is in danger—despite my having a witness to yesterday's attack—I've made the decision to hire private detectives."

That finally got Sissy's attention. She and Jonah looked at each other. Ami and Ned looked at each other. Gilda reached for the wine decanter.

Enzo said, "Private detectives? Without even telling me?" He sounded wounded.

"Good for you, darling," Wynne said. There was a hint of mischief in her sparkling black eyes as she glanced at the Nevins. They seemed frozen in place. Jonah still held the serving spoon, noodles dangling, and Sissy stared at him like someone practicing mind control.

Horace ignored them all, pointing at Perry and Nick. "You've already met Nick Reno and Perry Foster. What you don't know is that they've agreed to stay at Angel's Rest until the mystery of who wants me dead is solved."

Perry threw Nick a quick *I-promise-you-I-did-not* look. Nick opened his mouth and closed it.

Ned said, "So that's why you have a gun."

"A *gun!*" Sissy and Jonah looked at each other in alarm.

Ami's expression was troubled. She said to Horace, "But if you really are in danger, shouldn't you call the police?"

"He's not in danger," Ned muttered. "He's playacting."

Cousin Sissy didn't wait for Horace's reply. "I never heard of anything so ridiculous," she exclaimed. "Not in all my born days. Who's going to pay these gentlemen's fees?"

"Not you," Horace retorted, "so you don't need to worry about it."

"I do need to worry about it because you have *no money*, Horace. As you're constantly telling us. These men are going to expect to be paid, and then what will happen? You can't expect me and Jonah to finance something so ridiculous as this."

"No, I can't—and I don't. It'll be a cold day in hell when I expect any support from you two."

"Well, I like that!" Jonah belatedly jumped into the fray. "After everything Sissy and I've done for you."

They exchanged another look of silent—albeit outraged—communication.

Enzo demanded, "What have you done but mooch off him?"

"If that isn't the pot calling the kettle black!"

Perry didn't like the funny little smile on Horace's face as he watched Enzo and the Nevins sparring. Was this all a ruse for Horace's entertainment? Not yesterday's attack, obviously. That had been real enough. But was Horace deliberately milking—dramatizing?—the events of the day before?

Maybe it wasn't even conscious on his part, given the things his unpleasant cousin had hinted at that morning.

"Wait a second, wait a second." Enzo broke off bickering with the Nevins and fastened a dark and beady eye on Perry. "That's quite a coincidence that *you* just happen to be waiting around for Horace to get assaulted by hooligans, and then you turn out to be a private dick."

"I'm not a PI," Perry answered. "Nick is. I work part-time in a library."

Nick said not a word. He might have been watching a play. A play he had been forced to attend.

"It's true," Horace cut in. "The boy is an *artist*. A true talent. One day you will all know his name!"

Ugh. So embarrassing. Leave it to Horace to make painting sound like some grandiose endeavor.

"We know his name now," Enzo retorted. "You already told us. Perry Foster. And it's the same difference if he's the dick or his boyfriend is."

Being a fan of vintage pulp novels, Perry knew that "dick" was just another word for PI, but somehow it sounded like something very different coming out of Enzo's mouth.

"I thought I was the paranoid one." Horace had that weird smile again, like he found all of this funny.

Enzo replied bleakly, "Just because you're paranoid doesn't mean they're not out to get you." He looked pointedly at Sissy and Jonah.

"How does this have anything to do with us?" Sissy demanded in answer to that look. "We've already said we're against the idea. The notion that Horace would hire private detectives is…is…"

"Ridiculous," Jonah supplied.

"Ludicrous," Sissy said.

"*No!*" Gilda cried.

That shut everyone up. They all turned to study Gilda, who had pushed back in her chair and was gazing ceilingward with a dreamy expression.

"There *is* danger here. Danger for Horace. Danger for all of us."

"That's right," Ned said. "It's living out in the old swimming pool and eating our leftovers."

Wynne laughed.

Enzo cried, "That's not true. I buy all Wally's food myself."

Gilda frowned and stopped looking for the stars amongst the ceiling beams. "This is nothing to scoff at. My visions are real. I've warned Horace. He's surrounded by enemies."

"Oh, for heaven's sake," Sissy said to Horace. "Enzo is right about one thing. You know nothing about this boy and his friend. He's a trespasser. That's all you know."

Horace said slyly, "I know he appreciates what none of you do!"

"Which is what?" Sissy looked from Horace to Perry.

"He appreciates my home. He appreciates my collections. Which is why—" Horace's gaze fell on Nick, who was watching him silently, steadily. He finished a little lamely, "He, er, appreciates the danger I'm in."

"I'll just bet he does!" Jonah said.

Perry felt himself go hot with anger and embarrassment. Not so much at what Jonah was implying—whatever the hell that might be—as what they would all think if and when they learned Horace had changed his will. Assuming Horace really had. Because why would he? It was a crazy thing to do.

Then again, according to Sissy and Jonah, Horace *was* crazy.

Perry's heart was pounding. He had to lower his voice to keep it steady. "You couldn't be more wrong," he said to Jonah. "I'd never even heard of Horace until yesterday."

"I forgive you for that," Horace said magnanimously.

Sissy made a smothered exclamation of impatience. "I'm not going to sit here and listen to any more of this nonsense." She rose with surprising alacrity, Jonah leaped to drag her chair out of the way, and Sissy left the table, the wind in her sails— or, more exactly, the draft in her muumuu. Jonah grabbed their plates and silverware and trotted after her.

As they vanished into the hallway, Horace said to Nick, "I find her behavior suspicious, don't you?"

"I find your behavior suspicious," Nick replied.

Surprisingly, everyone, including Horace, laughed. But Perry knew Nick wasn't kidding.

Wynne said, "Was that the end of your announcement, darling? Our wonderful food is getting cold."

"Yes," Horace said. "That was it." He sat back down. He seemed a little let down.

Ned Duke laughed again and said to Perry, "No good deed goes unpunished."

Which was what Nick had said that morning when they hiked down to the main highway to retrieve their bags after the meeting with Horace.

Nick had not been happy then, and he was less happy now. Perry was going to have to figure out some way to make this—

His thoughts broke off as something slammed into the window behind him. Hard.

Wynne squealed. Nick's hand fastened on Perry's shoulder as though he was about to shove him under the table. Proof of how on edge everyone's nerves were, Nick wasn't the only one on his feet.

"A bird!" Ned exclaimed shakily. "A crow, I think. I saw it hit the window."

"Are you sure?" Horace looked terrified, eyes raking the darkness behind the glass.

Nick was already striding down the row of towering windows, heading for the door that led onto the terrace.

Perry pushed his chair back and started after him. He was joined by Ned and Ami. Together they crowded out through the segmented glass door and onto the leaf-piled terrace, staring around themselves. The night was unexpectedly cold. Wind shook the nearly bare tree branches, sending twisted, crooked silhouettes wavering against the walls. The moon cast an ominous greenish light over the urns and white iron tables and chairs.

Through the windows they could see the others still seated at the table. It looked as though Horace and Wynne were arguing. Gilda sipped her wine and stared into space once more. Looking for answers in the stars, or watching for the next off-course bird?

Enzo gazed out the windows, though it was doubtful he could see them moving around on the terrace.

"The crows have a nest in the east tower. It must have got confused in the wind. There." Ami pointed to a black and shapeless darker shadow a foot or so from where Nick stood.

Nick nudged the shadow with the toe of his boot. "It's a raven, not a crow. You can tell by the neck hackles."

"A raven." Ned gave a nervous laugh. "Aren't those bad luck?"

"Is it still alive?" Ami asked.

"Nope."

Something brushed against Perry's face. He looked up. The last of the autumn leaves swirled down from overhead. In the weird light, they looked candy-colored: grape, lime, cherry, lemon. Sort of pretty, sort of poisonous.

A scrape of sound carried from the arched doorway leading into the small courtyard where he'd found Horace yesterday afternoon. He stared across the piles of leaves and the broken furniture and saw—*wait.*

Was that…? His hair prickled on his scalp. Yes.

The gleam of eyes.

Perry said, "Nick—" as one of the shadows detached itself from the wall and backed slowly, cautiously down the steps.

At the same time, Ami pointed toward the doorway. "There's someone there. Someone is in the courtyard!"

The watcher in the shadows turned, abandoning any attempt at stealth, and ran, feet crunching through the dead leaves.

"Stay here, all of you," Nick ordered, and dived into the windswept darkness after the intruder.

CHAPTER SIX

The cold, clear night air was bracing after the musty, mothy fug of the interior. The adrenaline flooding Nick's bloodstream gave him the fuel to clear the terrace in a couple of strides. Action, *any* action, was a relief after a day spent wandering around the rubble of the hotel grounds and listening to old Horace babble about his Hollywood glory days. Horace didn't need a PI, he needed a shrink. Nick almost would have preferred sitting on a stakeout. Except there was no Perry on stakeout.

Even so.

Bad idea, Reno. You don't know who else is out here. You don't know if he's armed with more than a sword this time.

He could hear the rattle of leaves, the snap of twigs beneath the intruder's feet as he ran through the courtyard—he was no more than two yards ahead of Nick as he burst out of the enclosure and fled down the stone steps leading to the garden.

Thanks to the sickly moonlight, Nick got a pretty good look at him then. The asshole was wearing a cape. Yep, a cape. His head was covered by something white. A rubber mask? Probably. Best guess? A skeleton mask. Credit where credit was due. This asshole had the balls to return to Angel's Rest so soon. And all by his lonesome too.

You are so mine.

The target made it down all three flights of stairs without tripping, turned left, and fled down another walkway. Where the hell was he headed? There was a gate leading to the back of the property only a few feet in front of him. Did he think he could hide in the greenhouse? The old swimming pool? Nick could hear him crashing through dead brush and dried shrubs, and he seemed to be moving with purpose, clearly familiar with the hotel grounds. Nick had memorized the general lay of the land, but there was a lot of acreage to cover. Meandering pathways and flights of steps leading nowhere complicated his pursuit.

His quarry had now reached the terraced hillside, scrambling up the dry slope like an energetic mountain goat, confirming Nick's belief that he was chasing someone young and male. Someone with an already mapped out plan of escape—and an exit strategy.

Which Nick now understood. The intruder knew better than to simply try to outrun him. Instead, he was trying to lose Nick by leading him through an obstacle course.

Sweating, breathing fast, Nick reached the top of the hillside. He was in good shape, though not like back when he'd been a SEAL, so yeah, this guy was definitely younger than him.

The man in the cape disappeared into a copse of dead trees. From not far ahead Nick heard the scrape of boots on rock, the *clink* of rolling bottles, the *clang* of something heavy and metal landing on stone.

He slowed his pursuit in time to avoid falling over the iron patio chair that had been placed directly in the middle of the brick path—and to sidestep the beer bottles that had been kicked onto the trail. It cost him valuable seconds.

Deciding to try and head the other off, he veered from the brick path, pushing his way through a mostly dead nine-foot hedge. He found himself on the edge of an empty field of weeds and rocks. With no trees or buildings to act as breaks, the wind whipped across the open space, stinging his eyes and filling his ears.

It seemed he wasn't the only one looking for shortcuts. The caped figure had opted for the same strategy. He was several yards ahead of Nick and covering the uneven terrain like an antelope, making for the chain-link fence at the back of the property. Nick threw on a last burst of speed and gained some lost ground.

Not enough.

If his quarry had had to climb the fence, he'd have caught him for sure. But instead, the target swerved left, disappearing behind a couple of scrub oaks—bent nearly in half with the force of the wind—and coming out on the other side of the chain-link where a small dirt bike was parked.

Nick reached the cut fence a few seconds too late. He watched, fuming, as the intruder straddled the bike and gunned the engine. Nick swore. The guy on the bike flipped him the bird and rocketed off into the night.

Nick swore again, watching the red taillight vanish down the dirt road like an errant spark.

Mission failed.

Hell, he hadn't even managed to get a license number.

Fuck.

He examined the cut fence. It was hard to tell in the moonlight and with chain link, but it did not appear to him that the fence had been cut recently. He was pissed at himself all over again for not discovering this point of entry when he'd walked the perimeter that afternoon.

Although, in fairness, there were countless points of potential illegal entry on the property. Mending the fence—which he would see about tomorrow—wouldn't guarantee keeping anyone out. Not if they were determined to get in.

He listened to the angry whine of the motorbike fading into the night sounds of katydids and crickets. He turned and walked back to the hotel. As he retraced his footsteps through the little garden where the intruder had tried to ambush him, he could hear the alligator bellowing its mating call from the old swimming pool area. Just another lonely old codger in a place overrun with them.

Nick sighed.

So what had been the point of that little exercise?

In fact, go back a day earlier. What had been the point of three punks dressed in skeleton costumes attacking Horace?

Horace had believed it was an attempt on his life, but how likely was that?

Perry didn't believe he had stopped an attempted homicide. According to Perry, he had run into the skeleton men on the stairs leading from the courtyard. In other words, they had finished with Horace and were making their escape. They had not killed Horace. They had not even hurt him very badly.

And what about tonight?

It seemed highly unlikely Horace would be in the habit of taking a moonlit stroll, so what had the intruder been waiting for? Had his mission simply been one of surveillance?

To what end?

By that point in his reflections Nick had reached the hotel's inner courtyard. He used the flashlight app on his phone to search the ground near the steps leading to the terrace. Sifting through the leaves, he found a mound of cigarette butts, some of them still warm. He did some quick calculations. At ten minutes a cigarette, their intruder had stood out here smoking for about an hour and a half.

Even with sunset at six p.m., that was pretty brazen. The guy had positioned himself no more than five yards from the dining-room windows.

Of course, if the bird hadn't flown into the window, he could have spent the entire evening watching them, and they would have been none the wiser. It was not a reassuring thought.

Nick went up the steps to the terrace. Through the tall windows he could see the residents of Angel's Rest milling around the table. They looked like actors unable to find their marks on a stage set.

Where the hell was Perry?

The uneasy question had only just formed when Perry said, "Nick?"

His slim, pale shadow crossed the terrace to meet Nick.

"Hey," Nick said. And then, "He got away." He was still chagrined. "He had a motorbike parked behind the back fence."

Perry did not seem surprised. "I tried to get Horace to call the police. He won't. This time he's got a bunch of witnesses, but still no. He flat out refuses."

Nick made a sound of acknowledgment. Perry was right to be concerned. Something was definitely wrong with this setup.

"Were you able to get a good look at him?" Perry asked. "*Was* it a him?"

Nick sighed his exasperation. "I'm pretty sure it was a him, but no. I didn't get a good look at him. And even if I had, he was in costume."

He could feel Perry's stare in the darkness. "Yeah." He answered Perry's unasked question. "A cape and a skeleton mask."

Perry seemed to think that over, making no move to return to the dining room. "You know what's weird about this?"

"Uh…everything?"

"*Especially* weird."

"No. What?"

"Well, if our theory is that this person is some kind of crazed fan, wouldn't you think he'd be dressed like someone from one of Horace's movies?"

"You haven't seen most of Horace's movies. How do you know he's not?"

"You've seen his movies. Was he?"

"Not that I recall, but those films all run together." He was not being critical. He had enjoyed the hell out of Horace's movies in his teens. But they did all pretty much run together. A lot of boobs. A lot of blood.

Perry was still thinking. "Horace spent all afternoon showing us movie stills and posters and lobby cards. I never saw anyone dressed like the guys I ran into yesterday. They're carrying wooden swords, so some kind of thought went into their costumes."

He was right. The choice of wooden swords was too impractical to be random.

Perry added, "And wouldn't you think someone obsessed with Horace's movies would focus on one particular film or character?"

"Maybe." That was an interesting angle. Leave it to Perry to offer that kind of unique insight. At the same time, it was hard to predict how a deranged brain might reason.

"Horace never pointed out any particular film as one that might have inspired these crazed fans. Which…wouldn't you think he would?"

Nick said, "He may not know which film. He may not remember. He made a lot of movies."

Over one hundred films in a relatively short career—a career interrupted by alcohol, drugs, and an extended stay in a mental-health facility. That last one was something Nick planned on finding a little more about.

"Even so," said Perry. "His most famous film is probably *Why Won't You Die, My Darling?* which I did see. It was set in the 17th century. It's about witch hunters. There aren't any skeletons. And even if there were, the costumes Horace's attackers were wearing were just ordinary modern skeleton outfits. You'd think people who were going to the trouble of stalking someone would be more obsessed with the details."

"You're making a lot of assumptions." Despite the seriousness of the situation, Nick was a little amused. "You can't judge based on the type of stalker you would be."

"Still. Vampires, monks, witches, zombies…any of those would make sense in the context of Horace's filmography. And, given the fact that it's almost Halloween, those are costumes that would be readily available too."

Hmm. That sounded like Perry had been checking out Halloween costumes. Had he been invited to a Halloween party? Had he planned on attending a Halloween party before Nick got home ahead of schedule?

And why would that be a problem?

It wouldn't be, and yet Nick didn't like the thought of it. At all.

He forced his thoughts back on track. "Okay. What do you think is going on, then?"

"I don't know," Perry admitted.

"Do you think these are just random guys wearing random costumes?"

Perry thought it over. "Do you?"

"No."

"Me neither. Horace has a good point about there being three of them."

Nick thought he could follow this line of Perry's reasoning. "One obsessed fan is understandable. A coordinated effort defies belief."

"Right. Exactly."

"It's not impossible, though. Old people get bullied too. It's not a nice thought, but sometimes people who seem a little odd or out there, get targeted. That could be happening here."

Even as he framed his argument, Nick felt unconvinced by it. Yes, it could be the case that Horace had come to the attention of a trio of young thugs who were having fun tormenting him. But according to Horace, the threats and attempts on his life happened every Halloween. As far as Nick knew, bullying was not a seasonal occupation.

The glass door opened, and Enzo said, "Horace wants to know what you're doing out here."

"Nothing. We're coming in," Nick said.

Enzo stopped Nick as he followed Perry through the door. Enzo's usually mournful brown gaze was suspicious, hostile. "I'm watching you."

"I don't charge," Nick said.

Enzo's face darkened. "What kind of a crack is that?"

What kind of crack did Enzo think it was? Nick didn't know or care. He was rapidly losing patience with all of Angel's Rest's guests, barring one. The one he planned on extracting as soon as possible.

He said curtly, "Take notes. Maybe you'll learn a thing or two," and left Enzo spluttering his indignation.

Back in the dining room, Perry was explaining to Horace and the others that Nick had been unable to catch the intruder. With the exception of Horace, everyone seemed disappointed but not surprised. Horace waved off the news of Nick's failure.

"He chased him away. That's the important thing."

Perry looked troubled. "Well…"

"It's not that simple," Nick said. "There's nothing to keep him—them—anyone from coming back. In fact, there's evidence to suggest they've created a regular path of entry onto the property."

Horace pursed his mouth and looked thoughtful.

"I strongly recommend you phone the police," Nick added, since Horace still didn't seem to get the message.

The more he thought it over, the more certain he was that this was not a simple case of stalking. Not that stalking cases were ever simple. But they weren't generally a group activity. A police presence might or might not act as a deterrent, but at the least it ought to give someone second thoughts.

Horace said, "I know you mean well, my dear boy, but the last thing we need is the fuzz poking around here."

The fuzz?

"Okay, then maybe you should think about hiring a bodyguard," Nick replied. "Which I'm not."

"Nick," Perry said.

Nick put up a hand. "Okay. Fine. I just want us to be on the same page. It's going to be hard for me to figure out what's going on here when I'm not getting much—or any—help from the client."

The Winthrop woman, who was making short work of an acre of lasagna, said, "Got it. You are not to be blamed if the old fool is murdered in his bed tonight. Now sit down and have your supper. You'll feel better. There's never been any use in arguing with Horace. He's as stubborn as a mule and only half as smart. And I say this as someone experienced in the ways of mules."

Perry was waiting for him to decide. Not that there was really any decision to make. He wasn't going to let Perry down. Or leave Horace to his fate, however deserved, if at all avoidable. Nick nodded, and Perry smiled, relieved and slightly apologetic, not that he had anything to apologize for. He was too kindhearted for his own good, but it was one of the things Nick loved about him.

Though he loved it less tonight.

They took their places at the table once more, and the wine bottle was handed their way. Nick topped up Perry's glass. Perry smiled at him. Nick's heart warmed and expanded the way it always did when Perry looked at him that way. Like Nick was his own personal knight in shining armor. He—Perry—was bound to get over thinking of Nick that way eventually, but it sure was nice while it lasted.

Gilda the Great suddenly piped up, intoning in a faraway voice, "Horace is not destined to die tonight. Nor in his bed—"

"Perfect. Then we can all relax for the evening." Winthrop reached for her wineglass, held it up. "Cheers, everybody!"

CHAPTER SEVEN

"I promise I'll make it up to you," Perry said as Nick locked the door to their room.

The Olive Garden could have learned a few things about never-ending pasta bowls from Ami Savitri, but dinner was finally over and the denizens of Angel's Rest had all retired to their coffins or wherever they slept at night. Nick and Perry had accompanied Horace in the birdcage elevator to the third floor, where they had a room a couple of doors down from Horace's apartment suite.

It had probably been a very nice room once upon a time. The ivory embossed wallpaper was peeling off in sheets, but the space was large and airy with a high ceiling and a mismatched collection of good quality antique furniture. The bed was the size of a small schooner, and the linens probably dated from the same era. They were clean enough, though, because Nick had insisted on bundling everything outside and spreading the sheets and blankets on the terrace to air them in the sun that afternoon. Two squat blue and silver striped chairs sat before a faux fireplace against the far wall. A tall indigo-blue vase held a bunch of faded plastic flowers. The room's most notable feature was a small crowd of mannequins dressed like witches in the corner next to the windows. That was likely more about storage than decor.

Nick laughed and took Perry into his arms. "Yeah? I'm looking forward to hearing all the details."

Perry whispered some of the details, and Nick groaned and kissed him deeply, wetly.

A few feet away, the wind rattled the windows in their casements. Perry started and then made a face. No way had Nick not noticed his jump, but he kindly ignored it. Perry said, "I hope they don't fall out during the night. The windows, I mean."

"I don't know. The night air might be better for you than the air in this closet." Nick was only half kidding.

Perry smiled, but he wished Nick wouldn't keep bringing up his asthma. He was trying to forget about the constriction in his chest, the choky feeling in his throat. He didn't want Nick feeling like he had to baby him.

The windows creaked in their frame at another gust of wind. It sounded like the ocean out there.

"Listen." Nick nuzzled him. "You didn't force me into anything, so stop feeling like you did. Horace is a kook, but I think your instincts were right. I think someone does mean him harm."

That was a relief, because Perry believed that Horace was in danger. Sitting at that table tonight, he had been conscious of deep and troubling undercurrents. Angel's Rest was cocooned in cobwebs and secrets.

"The main thing is we get to spend the weekend together," Nick said.

Perry brightened. That was how he felt, but it was a relief to know Nick felt the same way. "Yes. True."

"Although if you did make other plans, that would be okay too."

"Huh?"

Nick said, almost painstakingly, "If I hadn't got back this weekend and you hadn't come here, if you'd wanted to go out for Halloween—go to a party with friends or something like that—that would be okay too."

"Yeah. Sure. But..." Perry shrugged. He did sometimes go out for a meal or coffee with friends. A party without Nick didn't sound like a lot of fun.

"Because," Nick labored on, "even though it won't always be like this, with me gone so much, it is like this for now. I don't really expect you to sit home alone every night."

"Oh. Okay."

Nick seemed weirdly earnest about this. Why? It wasn't like it was the first time they'd had this conversation. Perry had told him he understood about Nick having to work the lousy shifts and take all the overtime he could get. He did miss Nick a lot when he was away, but that was normal. He assumed Nick missed him just as much. In fact, he knew Nick did.

"I know it's got to be boring for you sometimes."

That surprised Perry. "*Boring?* No. Not at all."

"No?" Nick studied him doubtfully.

Perry shook his head, a little surprised that Nick didn't know this. "No. Between school and work, it's already hard to find time to paint. And I'd rather paint when you're gone anyway, so I can just relax and concentrate and not feel like I'm missing out."

"Missing out?"

"On spending time with you."

Nick gave a funny groan and scooped Perry up the way he did sometimes, carrying him over his shoulder to the bed and dropping him onto the mattress.

Perry laughed up at him. He loved it when Nick got playful and pretended to roughhouse him. Underneath his hard exterior, Nick was a very gentle guy. Although when Perry had told him so, Nick had burst out laughing and said, "Only with you, kiddo. Only for you."

It was one of the few times Perry hadn't minded being called "kid."

Now Nick knelt on the bed, shoving up Perry's shirt and tracing the lines of Perry's ribs with his fingertips. He looked almost solemn—probably about to deliver another sermon on nutrition. Perry reached up, held Nick's head so he had to meet Perry's eyes. He brushed Nick's hard cheekbones with the edge of his thumbs.

"I'm fine. Stop worrying about me. I'm happy so long as we're together."

"We're always together," Nick said gruffly. "Even when we're apart, we're together." His face was turning red—he almost never said things like that, and Perry felt a surge of pro-tective tenderness.

"I want to paint you, Nick."

Nick groaned. "Not that again."

"Again? I've never done it. Only sketches. That's not the same thing."

"I can't sit still that long," Nick said, which wasn't true. He did get restless, though.

Perry opened his mouth, but Nick ended the conversation by putting his head down and suckling the point of Perry's nipple. His mouth was warm, his lips so very soft, especially in contrast to the rough velvet of his five—make that ten—o'clock shadow. Perry gulped and stretched, flexing his back and rubbing at the growing bulk at his own groin.

"So sweet," Nick mouthed against him. His tongue rasped pleasurably against Perry's almost painfully sensitive nipple. "Candy from my baby."

That was a little joke. The ten years between them had initially worried Nick, and consciously or unconsciously, he had said and done some distancing things. Thank God he was over that. Perry had been twenty-three when they met. He was not remotely a child.

"Yes…" Perry closed his eyes, concentrating on the wet heat of Nick's tongue flicking so delicately, deliciously at the taut points of his nipples. He whispered, "I like that."

Really, there was nothing he didn't like. Nothing they'd tried so far anyway. Nick was both indulgent and demanding when they made love—and it was always lovemaking with them—so much better than anything, any*one*, Perry had dreamed of for all those years.

Nick knelt between his thighs, taking Perry's throbbing cock in one hand and his aching balls in the other. Nick's cock was thrusting up, swollen and dark against the hard, taut planes of his belly, but he was in no hurry. He never rushed this. Any of it.

Outside, the wind was pounding against the windows, but Perry felt safe and warm and happy. Nothing mattered but this moment with Nick.

Then Nick froze. His head shot up, listening. Perry heard it too. Someone was knocking softly on the door of their room.

Perry swore softly.

The tapping came again, a soft, almost nervous sound—although that was probably Perry's imagination. You couldn't tell from a knock if someone was nervous. He just took it for granted that anyone wandering around Angel's Rest at night would be jumpy.

"Why am I not surprised?" Nick did a one-hip bounce off the mattress and grabbed his jeans. He was in them in two steps and opening the door on the third. Perry threw the bedspread over his lap—and then grabbed a pillow for good measure.

Horace stood on the other side of the door, blinking at the *whoosh* of air caused by Nick throwing the door wide. He wore a sumptuous black-and-orange kimono, as though he was starring in a Halloween version of *The Mikado*. His hair was scraped back in an almost ferociously neat ponytail.

Holding up a square crystal decanter of amber liquid, he said, "The good stuff. How about a nightcap?"

Not an emergency, then. As sympathetic to Horace as Perry was, he could cheerfully have strangled him right then. Nick was looking at him in inquiry. It was a serious question. Nick was more than capable of telling Horace thanks, but no thanks.

But the fact that Horace had turned up this late—and with a bottle of booze—made Perry think that just maybe, he was finally ready to talk. Or at least might, after a drink or two, be open to answering a few questions honestly. So Perry said quickly, "Sure," as if there was nothing he wanted more than to spend yet another hour listening to Horace.

Nick sighed, gave the door a little push, and it swung open with a haunted-house creak. Horace swept in with an airy, "*Grazie*, dear boy. *Grazie*."

Nick's face was expressionless as he closed the door.

"How's the room?" Horace asked vaguely, glancing at the dusty furniture and mob of black-clad mannequins. "Comfortable? Did you find everything you needed?"

Without waiting for their reply, he dropped into the chair next to the faux fireplace, deposited the three tumblers he was carrying on the small side table, and splashed an inch of golden liquid into each one. He picked up the nearest glass, sketched a salute, and said, "Cheers."

Then he stared into the fireplace's firebox as though there really was a grate and flames flickering there.

Nick wandered over, picked up the other two glasses, and carried them to the bed. He handed one to Perry and then perched on the foot of the mattress, studying their uninvited guest.

Perry sniffed his glass. Whisky probably. One of his least favorite drinks in the world. Partly because Nick was always trying to get him to drink "hot toddies" when he thought Perry was chilled or needed "beefing up." The recipe for that ghastly concoction of water, whisky, herbs, and honey had been handed down by Nick's granny, who was apparently the only member of his family he had fond memories of.

Nick waited, sipping his whisky. His brows shot up, so maybe it *was* the good stuff.

Perry took a cautious sip and grimaced inwardly. Nope. No whisky was the good stuff. He much preferred cocktails made with fruit juice and rum.

"What's on your mind?" Nick asked finally.

Horace glanced over as if surprised to find them still there.

"Ah." He took a belated swallow of his own drink. "Well. It's only that I thought about what you said at dinner. It's true. That is, I may have not been entirely…forthcoming this afternoon."

Nick's smile was grim. "You weren't forthcoming at all." He took another swallow of whisky.

Blunt but accurate. Horace had spent the entire afternoon talking, but had managed to avoid ever saying anything to the point. He had gossiped about his fellow actors, he had recounted some amusing on and off set antics by his least favorite director, he had talked about the making of *Why Won't You Die, My Darling?* He had reminisced about getting drunk, getting stoned, getting beaten up, getting arrested. He had talked about the business manager who had cheated him and the business manager who had made him rich. He had talked about his plans for the museum that was never to be. He had talked and talked and talked.

Horace cleared his throat. "The trouble is, I do have…an inkling of who is behind these threats."

"An inkling? Does this inkling have a name?"

"Troy. Troy Cavendish. We were friends once."

Perry remembered Sissy referring to someone named Troy. She'd said something about a stabbing—and that Troy had brought it on himself.

Nick asked, "Troy Cavendish? Is that a stage name?"

Horace nodded. "He was an actor. For a time. He had a part in one of my films. *Zombies of the Last Judgment*."

"*Zombies of the…*"

Nick didn't bother trying to hide his distaste. Horace said haughtily, "My films were not great art, perhaps. But they entertained."

"Sure," Nick said indifferently. Perry refrained from volunteering the information that his parents had banned Horace's movies.

Horace, lost in his memories, smiled faintly. "Troy wasn't very good, but he was *very* pretty. We became...close."

"What happened?" Perry asked.

"I don't know really." Horace sighed. "Maybe it was the booze, the pills, the pressure. I was working a lot, and he felt I could—should—do more to help his career." Horace fell silent. "Maybe I could have," he murmured sadly after a moment.

Nick said, "What was Troy's real name?"

Horace squinted at some distant recollection. He said finally—and he was looking and speaking to Perry, "It wasn't like it is now. We couldn't be like you are with him."

Perry nodded. He knew. Old people tended to confide in him. Apparently, he had one of those faces. He knew that even during the legendary sexual revolution, most of the country had still held very narrow views of homosexuality.

"It would have damaged my career—and I was already doing plenty of that on my own." Horace smiled with unexpected charm. Then his smile faded. "But Troy didn't believe that. He kept pushing for more and more. I couldn't give him what he wanted."

"How long ago was this?" Nick questioned. "It had to be a while back."

"It would have been the seventies. '78? '79?"

Nick sighed. "You're telling me you believe this Troy Cavendish has been trying to kill you every Halloween since 1978?"

"I know it sounds strange."

Nick's eyebrows rose. He glanced at Perry. Perry tried, without words, to urge Nick to let Horace tell his story in his own way. He knew there was more to this. A lot more. There had to be if decades later, Horace was still getting choked up about it.

"It was Troy's idea to buy Angel's Rest. It was still running as a hotel back then, though its heyday years were long past. And it was his idea to start a museum with the memorabilia I'd collected through the years. I can't say he had a head for business, but he was very clever."

"How long were you together?" Perry asked.

"Three years. A little more than three years."

"How did it end?"

"Badly. As we began to grow further apart, Troy became involved with a local group of…I suppose you would have to call them occultists. He began to dabble in black magic and sorcery."

"Satanism?" That was Nick. Satanism was about the extent of Nick's knowledge of the occult. Perry, on the other hand, had gone to high school with kids who openly identified as witches or Wicca.

"Perhaps. He denied it, but perhaps. He became more and more enmeshed with them."

"And you argued over his, er, religious beliefs?" Nick asked.

"Yes. Often. But that wasn't what broke us up." Horace turned back to the nonexistent fire and stared moodily at the wall.

"What broke you up?"

Horace closed his eyes, shook his head. He opened his eyes. "I had decided to marry Wynne. Troy came home one morning after one of their séances or summonings—whatever they were doing—and found us in bed."

Perry had to bite his lip at Nick's expression. This had to be a new twist on cheating-spouse cases.

"Wynne?" Nick repeated. "Wynne Winthrop? The woman who lives downstairs? The one we met at dinner?"

"Yes. Wynne and I have been great friends for years. We worked together a lot. She was my costar in *Why Won't You Die, My Darling?* Prudence is the only character who survives, if you recall." When neither Perry nor Nick recalled, Horace forged on. "The gossip rags always linked us together—not unfairly. She was in love with me back then, though she knew I was gay. Before Troy, we used to share a bed when we were between partners."

"That would make you bisexual, not gay," Nick said. He was a stickler for details.

"Whatever. I digress." Horace shuddered. "When Troy found us in bed, he...went crazy. He tried to kill us both. I got the knife away from him—"

Horace broke off, blinking like someone who had just woken from a trance. "I never saw him again."

Clearly, there was a lot of story missing between *I got the knife away from him* and *I never saw him again.*

"How is that possible?" Perry asked.

Horace didn't appear to hear.

"Where's Cavendish living now?" Nick was brisk.

"I don't know."

Maybe Horace really hadn't checked the return address on those threatening letters. Or maybe there hadn't been a return address.

"But you're sure he's the one sending you these letters?" When Horace nodded, Nick pressed, "Why? Were they signed?"

"Oh no! Certainly not."

"Was there anything specific in the letters that made you believe the author had to be Cavendish?"

Horace looked confused. "No. I don't think so. But who else could it be?"

"When did the first letter arrive?"

"I don't remember. Years ago."

"Forty years ago?"

"No. No, maybe five years ago."

"And that's when the attempts on your life began?"

"Yes."

"You just said Cavendish has been trying to kill you since 1978."

Horace grew flustered. "He first tried in 1978. He tried to stab me, as I just told you."

"Did he try again before the letters started five years ago?"

"N-no. I don't believe so." Horace seemed unsure. Wasn't it an odd thing not to be certain of?

"Okay. Cavendish tries to kill you in '78. Then nothing happens until five years ago when the threats and the...what? Accidents? Start up again."

Perry knew exactly what Nick was thinking. Why would Troy Cavendish wait so long to start sending threatening letters? And yet sometimes it did happen that way. Nick had told him about a case where a man had only started stalking his ex-girlfriend after he'd lost his job and his wife had divorced him. Of course, that had only been two years, not nearly forty.

"Yes." Horace answered Nick. He sounded a little testy.

"Just making sure I've got the whole story," Nick said. "How were these accidents arranged? What kind of accidents were they?"

"How should I know how they were arranged!"

Nick remained patient. "What kind of accidents were they?" he asked again.

"The giant carved headboard on my bed came loose and nearly crushed me. The chandelier over the dining table came down. The wiring in my bathroom—"

"It's an old building. Did you have someone come in and examine the wiring and the light fixture and the bed?"

"No!"

"Why not?" Nick asked reasonably. He was not being unkind, but it was not pleasant to watch him dismantle Horace's story. Horace was getting more and more rattled.

"They would have claimed I did it myself. For attention."

Perry questioned, "Who would?"

"The police. The electricians. Those vultures Sissy and Jonah. But I *know* these were genuine attempts on my life. No, I can't prove it. Yes, they were supposed to look like accidents. But I ask you, *why* would these things only happen to me? Why would they only happen in *my* rooms?"

If that was true, it was a fair question. But was it true? How reliable a witness was Horace?

Judging by Nick's reaction to Horace's story, not very.

"Who was the man watching the house tonight?" Nick questioned. "That wasn't any seventy-year-old."

"I don't know. How should I know? I didn't see him."

Nick studied Horace as though trying to decide if he believed him or not. "And what's Cavendish's real name?"

Horace hesitated, seemed to make his mind up. "Tom Ciesielski."

"There can't be too many of those in the phone book," Nick remarked. He rose. "All right. Thank you for sharing this information. I'll start following this lead tomorrow."

That was Horace's cue, but he didn't move. He looked at Nick and then Perry. "I did love him," he said. "I really did."

"Sure you did," Nick replied.

Nick had had to hide his sexuality during his years in the military, but he seemed to have no sympathy for Horace. Maybe his coolness stemmed from his distaste for Horace's cheating on Troy. Nick did not have much patience for cheaters. Added to that was the fact that Horace was a difficult personality: demanding, melodramatic, and completely self-absorbed.

Maybe Horace *was* playacting most of the time, but just for a moment, Perry thought he saw the glitter of tears in the old man's eyes.

CHAPTER EIGHT

"**I** think he still loves Troy," Perry said after Nick locked the door behind Horace and returned to bed.

"If you want to call that love." Nick was brusque. He didn't want Perry growing melancholy over Horace's tragic past. Most of the tragedy had been brought on by Horace's poor life choices.

Perry tipped his head, thinking. What Nick always thought of as his Christopher Robin look. "I don't see how Troy could be behind all this, though. He can't be sneaking into the hotel every year, let alone living here in disguise. It was forty years ago. He might not even be alive."

"Agreed," Nick said.

"I mean, I can see why Horace would make the connection, and Troy *could* be sending the letters, though it's weird he would wait so long—and what would be the point? The creepy skeleton costumes do kind of tie in with the occultist theme, but…"

"Yeah," Nick agreed. "The whole thing is very unlikely." He met Perry's troubled gaze, and made a face. "I promise to find out what happened to Troy Cavendish aka Tom Ciesielski. Okay? Word of honor. In the meantime, where were we before we were so rudely interrupted…"

Nick jerked awake.

It said a lot about how much his life had changed over the last year that he was less alarmed by screams in the middle of the night than he was the sound of Perry starting to wheeze.

Between the dust and damp, the ghosts and goofballs, the miracle was Perry hadn't had an asthma attack before now.

He sat up. One part of his brain was calculating where the screams were coming from. *Downstairs. West wing.* The other part of his brain was focused on what was happening with Perry. He felt around the bedding, finding the sheets warm where Perry had lain. "You okay?"

A dumb question because he could hear Perry knocking things off the bed stand as he scrabbled for his rescue inhaler.

Nick reached for the lamp on his side of the mattress, but when he pulled the chain, the light did not come on.

He yanked again. Nothing. The room stayed shrouded in darkness. "What the hell?"

Meanwhile, someone was still screaming in the nether regions of the house.

"Go," Perry gulped between the quick plastic *clicks* of his inhaler. "*Go.*"

"*Fuck.*"

The last thing he wanted to do was leave Perry in distress, but something sure as hell was happening outside this room.

He crawled over the tangle of sheets and blankets, finding Perry, who was sitting on the edge of the mattress. He gripped his bony shoulder hard, in what he hoped was reassurance. "Can you hang on a couple of minutes? I'll be right back."

He felt Perry's hurried nods.

"Slow, deep breaths, all right? Just stay calm, and—"

Perry exhaled sharply and wheezed, "Will...you...*go*?"

Nick rolled off the bed, landing on his feet, and grabbed his pistol. He felt his way across the floor and out into the drafty hallway.

The screams had stopped, but he could hear agitated voices drifting up the elevator shaft from downstairs. He ran down the hallway, pausing to thump on Horace's door.

Horace must have been listening to the shrieks from below too because his door opened a crack. Nick could see a pale blur—Horace—peering anxiously out. He quaked, "What is it? What's happening? Is he here?"

"I don't know. Lock this door and don't open it until I come back. Do you understand?"

In answer, Horace slammed shut the door and locked it.

And locked it.

And locked it again.

Nick heard a slide bolt, a dead bolt, and a turn bolt all shoot home in quick succession.

Assuming no one kicked in the door, he should be safe enough in there.

Nick raced down the hall, past the hooded monk, jumped in the elevator, and banged on the button. The metal cage lurched down a couple of floors, landing with a teeth-rattling bounce on the ground floor. Raised voices reached him from down the hall, but it sounded as though the crisis was over.

Nick shoved his pistol in the back of his waistband, scraped back the gate, and loped down the moonlit hallway.

Halfway down the drafty corridor he spotted a huddle of bathrobes and housecoats illuminated in the silvery light pouring through the Palladian windows.

"…probably forgot to pay the electric bill again," Sissy was saying as Nick joined the edge of the group. She was wearing a long shiny robe that made her look like she was encased in metal tubing. "Well, you took your time," she said, spotting Nick. "Lucky it wasn't a real emergency."

"What the hell's going on down here?" Nick demanded.

"It was W-W-Wally," Ami said between chattering teeth. She pointed in the direction of her room, but it was too dark to see whatever she was indicating. "He tried to get in again."

"He's got a crush on you," Nick said. He was unamused, though. Maybe there was a funny side to this, but it was a dangerous situation, no mistake.

Ami gave a laugh that sounded more like a sob.

"This can't go on," Duke said. Even in the dark, it was clear he had a serious case of bed beard going on. "What if that monster had got in?"

"Where's Enzo?"

"Where's Horace? That's the real question," Jonah said.

Nick said, "Mr. Daly is locked in his rooms upstairs."

"Enzo's taking Wally back to his pen," Duke said. "For all the good it's going to do, since he's figured out how to unlock the gate."

That afternoon Nick had taken a good hard look at the gate leading to the old pool yard. There was no way in hell that alligator had figured out how to work a padlock. Either Enzo had once again left the yard unlocked, or someone had deliberately, knowingly, let that lizard loose.

A little mischief-making on the part of their friendly, neighborhood skeleton men? Or something else?

"How did it get in here?" Nick surveyed the segmented arched doorway leading to the terrace. As far as he could tell, the door did not appear to be damaged. Nor were any of the windows broken. So how the hell was that gator getting inside the building?

No one answered.

"Isn't this door kept locked?"

"Yes. Of course," Sissy said. "Someone would have to open it. Someone crazy."

"Did anyone go out tonight?"

Once again no one spoke.

The glass door suddenly rattled, and alarm rippled through the group.

Ami's shadow sagged. "*Enzo*," she said in relief.

The bulky square of Enzo's shadow entered on a blast of night-scented air. "It's all right," he announced. "He's locked in again. I don't know how he got out."

"You left the gate unlocked is how he got out," Duke said.

"The hell I did! Not after this morning."

"For God's sake, let's worry about it in the morning," Wynne Winthrop drawled. She was wearing what appeared to be silk men's pajamas. "Sleep tight, everyone. Don't let the alligator bite."

Her tall silhouette sauntered down the hallway before seeming to dematerialize. The others began murmuring their good nights and departing to their rooms.

Enzo turned to Nick. "It wasn't me. I didn't forget. Not this time."

"I believe you," Nick said. And he did.

Horace began unlocking the door as soon as Nick knocked.

"All clear," Nick said as the door swung open. "It was the gator again. Also, the power seems to be out in places."

"I paid the bill!"

"Yeah, it's not that. It could be electrical problems."

Horace groaned.

"And you're going to have to do something about that reptile because it nearly took down the girl's front door this time."

"That's impossible! How would it get in? The pen is padlocked. The hotel doors are kept locked at night."

Nick was in a fever of impatience to get back to Perry. "No idea. But I saw Savitri's door. That thing wanted in. Another couple of minutes and it would have *been* in."

He left Horace huffing and puffing and insisting that it could not have been the alligator—what did he imagine, giant rats? Not that Nick would have been surprised to find the hotel was home to giant rats—and returned to his own room.

At first glance it looked like the bed was empty and a crowd of people were standing motionless by the windows. The hair rose on his scalp. Then Nick remembered the coven of mannequins. One of the figures moved.

"Is everything okay?" Perry asked. He had opened one of the windows and was standing in front of it, outlined in moonlight.

Nick went to him. "What are you doing? You're going to freeze." He wrapped his arms around him. Perry's skin was cold. Even his hair felt chilly.

"I'm okay." Perry's voice was hoarse. "I had to have some fresh air. What's happening downstairs?"

"False alarm."

"What was it?"

"The swingin' alligator of the pool yard went to visit the Savitri girl again."

"*Again?*" Perry turned his head to try to read Nick's face. "Is she okay?"

"She's fine. The door held. They built to last in the '20s."

"But *why*? Is she keeping a meat locker in her rooms? Why's that alligator want in there so much?"

"I'm guessing she's the only resident doing any real cooking in her apartment."

"How did it get in the hotel?"

"That's the question for the ages." Nick guided Perry back to bed, crawling in beside him and dragging the bedclothes over their shoulders. "How are you doing, kiddo? Are you warm enough?" He gulped as Perry's icy feet brushed his, then manfully folded Perry's feet between his own.

Perry huffed at the "kiddo" comment. Nick meant it affectionately. He loved and respected Perry. But there was no use pretending that decade between them wasn't real. It was.

"Fine."

Nick's lips twitched at that glum comment. His concerns about Perry spending the night in this rathole had been confirmed, but saying *I told you so* wasn't going to make things better. He slid an arm beneath Perry's shoulders, drawing him closer still and settling his head more comfortably.

"Why are the lights not working?" Perry asked, a frown in his voice.

"I don't know. God knows what the wiring is like in this mausoleum. The elevator is working, so it isn't that Horace forgot to pay the utilities."

Perry was silent for a minute or two. Nick hoped he was falling asleep, but he said suddenly, "Why would someone let that alligator inside?"

"We don't know that they did."

Perry said grimly, "Don't we?"

Surprise held Nick silent. Perry was right. There was no possible way for that alligator to have accidentally gotten out of a locked pen and into a locked hotel, so why was he still trying to come up with plausible scenarios? There were none. The only real question was the one Perry had just posed. *Why?*

Well, and *who*?

Perry sighed. "I'm sorry, Nick. I didn't think it would be this…"

"Bad?"

Perry groaned, and Nick laughed.

"It's okay. I've slept in worse places—and with a lot worse company." He kissed Perry's forehead and then the middle of his nose and then his upper lip. Perry chuckled, kissed him back, but his laugh was tired, subdued.

"Let's grab whatever sleep we can," Nick said, and Perry nodded.

Slowly, his body relaxed into the warmth of Nick's, and Nick was sure he was drifting off, but he said suddenly, wearily, "I miss Vermont."

Nick's heart stopped.

But fair enough. Unlike Nick, he had not spent half his life roaming the globe. Until California, the farthest he'd ever been from home was Burlington. It was natural he might feel a little homesick.

"Me too," Nick admitted. "I even miss the snow. I never thought I would."

"Yeah?" Perry tilted his face up as though trying to read Nick's expression.

Nick nodded. Searched his soul. Made himself say, "If you want to go back and see your folks for Christmas, I'll figure out a way to make it happen."

Improvise, adapt, and overcome.

Perry said doubtfully, "Would you be able to come too?"

"No. Not this year."

"Then no way. I'm not spending Christmas without you."

"I appreciate that. But if you really want to go…"

Perry lifted his head, said incredulously, "Are you saying you don't care if I'm not here for Christmas?"

Nick growled. "Of course I *care*. That's not what I'm saying. But if you're feeling homesick—"

"*You're* my home."

It closed Nick's throat. For a moment he couldn't get any sound out. Finally, he squeezed out, "Okay. Same."

Perry snorted. "You old romantic, you."

Nick kissed him and kissed him twice more for good measure. Perry chuckled, enjoying the attention. They lay quietly, holding each other. Nick was thinking.

He said slowly, cautiously, "There is a possibility. It wouldn't happen right away, but I could push for it to happen sooner than it might otherwise. Business is good. People like the idea of hiring ex-Navy-SEALs when they've got a problem. Roscoe has been talking about expanding, maybe eventually opening an eastern branch. He's even hinted around, wondering whether I might be open to moving across country again."

Perry sucked in a quick breath, and Nick hastened to add, "It wouldn't be for another year or two. And it might not be Vermont, but it would be a hell of a lot closer than we are now."

"*Yes*," Perry said. "That would be great."

"And it *might* be Vermont," Nick said. "Vermont was one of the possibilities being kicked around."

"That would be *great*," Perry said again. "It's fine if it takes a couple of years. It gives us a goal. Something to plan for."

Yes. Not just a dream, a real plan for a future they would build together.

"You could finish art school here while we save up to buy a house. A nice house. With an art studio for you and a big backyard for me."

"I didn't know you wanted a big backyard."

"Yeah. With a firepit and a toolshed."

Perry started laughing.

"What's so funny about that?"

He shook his head. "Just the way you said *a firepit and a toolshed*. So…soulful."

Nick laughed self-consciously. But he liked hearing the happiness in Perry's voice. They were both happy. Nick liked this plan a lot. Liked even more that Perry was willing—wanted—to invest in this dream.

"How am I so lucky?" Perry whispered, which had to be the nicest thing anyone had ever said to Nick. Within another minute or two Perry was sleeping, his breathing soft and steady. Nick could feel the curve of Perry's smile pressed against his throat.

For a time, Nick listened to the mice in the walls gnawing the woodwork, and mulled over their rosy plans for the future. Eventually he went back to wondering what the hell was going on at Angel's Rest. He was worried about Perry too. Less than twenty-four hours in this dump, and he had already had a second asthma attack. This was not a good place for him.

And what the fuck with the alligator? Whoever was letting that thing loose was taking a hell of a chance on someone being badly hurt. There had to be a reason for it, and as much as Nick would have liked to believe it was some well-intentioned idiocy like allowing a caged animal its freedom, he was pretty sure that wasn't the case. The intent was malicious.

Did it have anything to do with the skeleton-clad intruders?

It seemed like a completely different strategy with maybe a completely different goal.

But what goal?

If the alligator had been trying to break down Horace's door, it might make sense, but Horace was safely out of reach on the third floor. Instead, the beast had gone after the girl. Twice. Did someone have a grudge against Ami Savitri?

If so, it would have to be someone inside Angel's Rest. Someone with access to Enzo's keys as well as keys to the hotel perimeter doors. For all Nick knew, that was everybody in the hotel.

He continued to mull over the possibilities.

What if the alligator was being used as a distraction?

A distraction for what?

Maybe he ought to go see if he could figure that out.

Double-checking that Perry was deeply, comfortably asleep, Nick edged slowly, carefully out of the bed, tucking the blankets around Perry and then packing pillows around him for good measure.

Perry stirred, muttered a drowsy inquiry, and sank back into his dreams.

Nick stepped soundlessly across the floor to the door, eased the door open, and stepped into the cold and drafty hallway.

By now it was nearly daybreak. Night was fading to a soft gray fuzz. He could just make out the squares of the macabre paintings and the hooded figure of the monk standing guard by the elevator.

Nick locked the door and considered his options. The elevator was going to be too noisy. Everyone in the place would hear him coming. No, there had to be stairs on this level. Stairs running up and down. Those would be his best bet.

He set off briskly in the opposite direction from the elevator.

It was a very long hallway, but at last he spotted the landing between the two separate flights of stairs.

His foot twisted as he stepped on something round and hard. He caught himself and bent to have a look. A marble. The kind used in games kids didn't play anymore.

This one looked like a devil's eye.

An escapee from Horace's collection?

Nick pocketed the marble and continued toward the head of the staircase. His gaze sharpened as he realized that the dark pool of shadow at the foot of the steps leading from this floor to the next level, was not a shadow. A body in a cape lay motion-less, face down on the carpet.

Nick's heart jumped in his chest. He had seen that broken sprawl too many times to mistake it for anything but what it was.

Death.

CHAPTER NINE

Someone squeezed his shoulder. Nick's voice said quietly against his ear, "Perry?"

Perry opened his eyes to a chilly and unfamiliar gloom. *Where the hell—?*

Oh, right. Angel's Rest, where he'd dragged Nick for the weekend—and where it was apparently impossible to sleep for more than an hour at a time.

Then the urgency beneath Nick's even tone sank in.

Perry turned his head. He could see the gleam of Nick's eyes.

"What is it?" Instinctively, he was whispering too.

"I just found a dead guy in a skeleton costume."

Perry shot upright. "*Where?*"

"Right down the hall. At the foot of the steps leading to the fourth floor. I think he might have fallen. I found a couple of marbles scattered down the staircase."

"Marbles?" This was confusing. He had a feeling it would be confusing even if he were wide-awake, which he was not. In fact, he wasn't one hundred percent sure he wasn't still dreaming. "What the hell would he be doing up here?" That was a rhetorical question because of course Nick would have no more idea than himself. He followed it up with another dumb question. "What do you think happened to him?"

Nick said patiently, "I think he might have slipped coming down the stairs. If you feel up to it, you should get dressed."

"Yeah, I'm fine. I'm…" Confused but racing to catch up. Perry threw back the bedclothes, and Nick handed him his jeans and a flannel shirt. Perry took his clothes, saying, "I hope the body doesn't disappear."

Nick was moving away, pressing numbers into his cell, but he looked up at that. "What?"

"Like at the Alston Estate. Remember?"

Nick gave a funny laugh. "I think from now on we should make it a rule not to stay in places built before 1960." He resumed making his call. "Yeah. My name is Nick Reno. I'm a private detective staying at the Angel's Rest hotel off Laurel Canyon. I just found a body on the third floor."

Silence on Nick's end.

"Unknown."

Another silence. Perry finished buttoning his shirt and began hunting for his socks. His fingers were unsteady with cold and nerves. Dead bodies were not a good start to any morning.

"Unknown. It looks like an accident. It looks like he slipped coming down the stairs."

Perry pulled on his socks and found his shoes during the pause that followed. Poor Horace. This was… Well, come to think of it, for all Perry knew, Horace might appreciate the attention. One thing for sure, it vindicated his fears. For another, and maybe it was kind of cold to even think it, but maybe this took care of Horace's problems. Or at least the immediate problem of someone threatening to kill him.

Nick finished his phone call, disconnected, and said, "I've got to wait for the cops downstairs. It might be a good idea if you stayed with Horace until they get here."

"Oh. Uh… Okay." He was not crazy about that idea. He'd have preferred to stick with Nick. Not because he felt unsafe. Because where Nick was, was where the action would be, and Perry felt sort of possessive about this, er, case.

As though reading his mind, Nick said, "I'm kind of curious about how a handful of marbles ended up on that staircase. Since Horace is the one with the antique toy collection, I'm guessing they belong to him. Though that doesn't explain how they got on the stairs."

"Do you think someone left the marbles there deliberately? In hopes of causing an accident?"

Nick said, "Horace seems to use the elevator to move around the hotel, so I don't think he could have been the intended target. I don't know that there *was* an intended target. I kind of doubt it. Unless—"

Perry had a sinking feeling he knew where Nick was going with this. "Unless Horace left them there?"

Nick nodded. "If Horace thought someone was getting inside the hotel at night, it's possible he came up with a home-made booby trap."

That seemed more the way a Navy SEAL would think than a man like Horace, but Perry didn't know Horace well enough to predict.

"If he did deliberately place the marbles on the stairs, would that be manslaughter? Criminal negligence?"

Surely not murder?

"There are extenuating circumstances," Nick said. "Horace was in fear for his life. The victim was trespassing— had probably committed breaking and entering, was possibly even attempting burglary."

"Or planning to murder Horace."

Nick grimaced. "The thing is, this kid—"

"*Kid?*"

"Late teens, early twenties."

"Oh no." Now Perry really did feel sick.

"Yeah. The problem is, he fell coming *down* the stairs from the fourth floor. You can tell from the way he landed. His left foot is lying on the first step."

Perry preferred not to think about the fact that a corpse was lying down the hall from them, but he didn't miss Nick's point. "He wasn't after Horace," he said.

"It doesn't look like it. I don't know what he was up to, but how could he miss the fact that no one lives up there? He couldn't. So what was he doing?"

"What were *you* doing up there?" Perry asked. "You left the room to go exploring while I was sleeping?"

"Yes. I locked you in," Nick answered briskly, but he was avoiding Perry's accusing stare.

"That's not really the point, Nick." Perry was getting mad imagining Nick being the one to slip on a marble and kill him-self falling down a staircase. "I'm not worried about me. What if something had happened to you?"

Nick did not actually roll his eyes, but it was aggravat-ingly close. "Okay, I don't want to argue with you. We don't have time. I had an idea about the power going out in specific grids, and I thought I should just check it out."

"Good initiative, bad judgment," Perry retorted, which is something his pop had used to say to him when his enthusiasm occasionally overrode his common sense.

Nick laughed. "Okay, Sarge. That's fair." He leaned over and kissed Perry. His mouth was warm, the kiss sweet—that was as much of an apology as Perry would get. Anyway, it was very hard to stay irked with someone who pressed a smiling kiss onto your mouth. "Will you stay with Horace while I deal with LAPD?"

"Yes."

"Thank you. I think this news will come better from you than the police."

Perry thought so too, though he didn't relish his job of bearer of bad tidings. He left Nick heading for the elevator and knocked softly on Horace's door.

A floorboard squeaked on the other side of the door. "Who is it?" Horace called warily.

"Perry."

He heard a series of locks being thrown, and the door opened. Horace studied him blearily. It seemed he had been up for a while because he was dressed in baggy black jeans and some kind of painted velvet shirt. He was unshaven and looked haggard in the light streaming from the large picture window. "The power is back on. I'm making coffee."

"That sounds great," said Perry, who never drank coffee.

He followed Horace into his apartment. A black-and-green afghan was crumpled on the velvet sofa. A pillow lay on the

floor. He deduced that Horace had been sleeping on the sofa—
and it probably was not a rare occurrence.

"Where's your friend?" Horace asked. There was a slight
edge to the word *friend*, though Perry couldn't think why.

"He's downstairs waiting—actually, that's what I wanted
to talk to you about. Something has happened."

"It's about time." Horace sounded bitter as he led the way
to the kitchen, which smelled comfortingly normal: coffee,
toast, and maple syrup.

"Something not good."

Horace went straight to a perfectly modern-looking coffee
machine and picked up the carafe. Perry's words registered.
Horace stared. "What?"

"One of the skeleton men got into the house last night.
Nick found him this morning."

"Found him? Found him where?"

"Found him dead," Perry said. "Down the hall at the
bottom of the stairs."

"Down the *hall*? *This* hall?"

"Yes." Perry was watching Horace to see…well, he wasn't
sure. Nick hadn't instructed him on what to look for; he'd just
said to observe Horace's reaction. Horace appeared perplexed
and alarmed. Which seemed a reasonable response in Perry's
opinion.

"Dead. You said dead?"

"Yes."

"But how could he be? Are you sure?"

"Nick is sure. Nick is—has experience."

"But *how*?" Horace's eyes flickered. "You said he was at the bottom of the stairs. Did he fall? Could one of his accomplices have pushed him?"

Now that was an interesting thought.

"Nick couldn't tell how he died. It seems like he was probably alone, but we don't know that either."

"No." Horace, clearly on automatic pilot, finished pouring the coffee. "Cream and sugar? A snort of whisky perhaps?"

"Cream and sugar," Perry said, hoping Horace would follow his cue.

Horace added cream and sugar to the cup and handed it to Perry, then asked, "Where is Nick? What happens now?"

"Nick's waiting for the police."

"The *police*?" Horace nearly dropped his own cup. He looked horrified.

"We had to call the police," Perry said, a little surprised at this reaction. What did Horace think was supposed to happen after finding a body?

"How could you do such a thing without speaking to me?"

"We had to. We didn't ha—"

"You should have allowed me to phone my lawyer first!" Horace was flushed, his eyes bright with anger.

"But—"

"Your loyalty should be to *me*. I won't accept anything less!"

Perry was both fascinated and apprehensive at the abrupt swing from confusion to utter rage. "That would look guilty," he pointed out.

For a moment he thought Horace was too angry to even hear him, but then Horace seemed to think this over. The frightening glitter faded from his eyes. He offered a twitchy smile. "You're right. I see. Yes. True. You're right."

Perry said nothing. He was still startled by Horace's reaction.

Horace smiled again, weakly. "I'm sorry for shouting at you, lovey. But you see, my experience with the fuzz has not been a happy one."

"Sure," said Perry, unconvinced.

"I've been betrayed so many times. Betrayed by people I thought I could trust."

That time Perry didn't offer a response. He couldn't help thinking that that attitude, paired with Horace's quick temper, made Horace more than capable of shoving someone down a staircase. He watched in silence as Horace doctored his coffee with a generous slug of whisky. Horace's hands were shaking a little as he brought the cup to his mouth.

Perry said, "What do you think the, er, intruder was doing up on the fourth floor?"

Horace looked blank. "How should I know? Setting a trap for me, I suppose."

"Do you go up to the fourth floor very often?"

"No. But he couldn't know that." Horace stopped. He asked in a different tone of voice, "How did he get in?"

"I don't know. Nick didn't say. Maybe he doesn't know either."

Horace studied Perry's face with odd intensity. "You trust Nick very much, don't you?"

"Yes. Of course."

"Why?"

"Why? Because he's…he's trustworthy."

Horace's face twisted. He shook his head. "No. You think that because you love him. But loving someone doesn't make them trustworthy. His love for you doesn't mean he won't fail you in the end."

Wow. This was a grim outlook on love and romance.

"It isn't just that Nick has never let me down. He doesn't let anybody down. If he gives his word, it's the same as if he signed a contract. He's...he has honor." It sounded kind of silly and self-important saying it, but it was true. Nick was a man of honor. He believed in integrity and commitment and loyalty and all that stuff that so many people seemed to think was old-fashioned.

Horace was not impressed. He sniffed. "So you say. He seems like a blunt instrument to me."

Perry was amused rather than offended. "He can be."

Horace was once again following his own thoughts. "I want to see him," he said, as though coming to a decision. "I *have* to see him."

"Nick? He'll—"

"Not *Nick*." Horace slammed his cup down and strode out of the kitchen. "I must see the dead man."

Perry set his untouched cup down and sped after him. "I don't think that's a good idea."

He was talking to himself. Horace had left the apartment, leaving the door standing wide.

Perry hurried to catch up. "Mr. Daly, this isn't smart. We—you—don't want to take a chance on contaminating the scene."

Horace ignored him, striding down the long, grim corridor like a racewalker in the home stretch.

"We might accidently introduce evidence that confuses the situation," Perry said. He was trying to be tactful, but really. Did Horace not *see*? "The last thing we want is for the police to think this wasn't an accident."

"We don't know it was an accident," Horace threw over his shoulder. "Perhaps his confederates turned on him. Perhaps the house turned on him."

The house? Uh…yee-ah.

"Either way, you don't want to take a chance of leaving any DNA—"

What the hell. It was pointless to keep talking. Horace was not going to be satisfied until he saw whatever it was he needed to see.

They were now three quarters of the way down the hall. Perry's stomach curled inside itself at the unpleasant smell drifting toward them. He knew what that was.

"There," Horace said. "He's still there."

Having experience with disappearing corpses, Perry understood Horace's relief.

He too spotted the dark form lying at the bottom of the staircase. He made himself keep walking. He did not want to see this, but Nick would expect him to watch Horace and take note of his reactions.

He sped up and reached the dead man as Horace did. They stared in silence. The man was facedown. He was not tall, but he was muscular. He wore a cheap nylon cape over black spandex running pants. His head was at a weird angle, and a white-and-gray rubber mask was pushed back on his yellow hair like a melted hat. One black-tennis-shoe-clad foot rested awkwardly on the bottom step.

Horace said nothing. He knelt, pushed the body onto its side, and examined the boy's waxy, gray face. Because, yeah, Nick was right. This guy was maybe nineteen. Perry ignored the curdling in his stomach and simply *looked*. Beneath the pushed-up mask was a not particularly intelligent face—in fairness, he'd probably looked better alive—slack mouth, rolled-back blue eyes, a mashed-in nose.

There was razor burn on his throat.

"Thank God, thank God," Horace's voice wobbled.

Perry stared as Horace wiped tears from his face. "Do you know him?"

Horace shook his head. "No. I've never seen him before. Not without his mask."

So why—?

But then he got it. Horace was relieved to the point of crying because this body did not belong to who he had feared.

The dead man was not Troy.

CHAPTER TEN

First on scene were a pair of salt-and-pepper uniformed cops who looked like they'd been dragged out of retirement for one last job. Officer Bruce was short and portly with features like a Russian nesting doll and a silver bowl-cut that looked better on eleven-year-old girls than middle-aged men. Officer Nolan was tall and dark and grim. He looked like one of those guys who leaves the military and goes into law enforcement, but can't help thinking of the public as The Enemy.

"So the old man finally killed someone," Nolan said by way of greeting when Nick let them through the grand main entrance.

"So I wouldn't jump to any conclusions," Nick returned. "The power went out last night. I think there's a good chance the intruder may have fallen down the staircase in the dark."

Bruce and Nolan gave him the weary smiles of veterans used to dealing with know-it-all-know nothings. The three of them went quickly through the formalities of what, where, when, and how.

"A PI, huh?" Bruce said when Nick had finished his recital. "And you've been hired to do what exactly?"

That's confidential sprang to mind, but not only was Nick not officially in Horace's employ, there was no way to keep most of the story from coming out. The most he could do for

Horace was try to control the spin. Best-case scenario was the cops determined accidental death and closed the book. There would still be publicity, and more crazies coming out of the woodwork, but that was still much, much preferable to a full-on investigation.

Nick felt pretty sure it *was* an accident.

But pretty sure was not one hundred percent certain. He'd have liked to be one hundred percent certain.

And even if the kid's death had been an accident, there was still the problem of the power going off and the alligator getting loose all at the same time a prowler had entered the hotel.

"The kid who fell down the stairs is dressed like a trio who assaulted Daly on his patio on Friday. I chased him—or someone dressed like him—off the property last night."

"Let's see the victim." Nolan snapped shut his notebook.

Nick escorted them to the third floor, waiting while they examined the body, then pointing out the marbles on the steps. Officers Bruce and Nolan held a scowling conference over the caped figure.

Nick was not privy to their conversation, and even if he had been, he was distracted by the realization that someone had moved the body since he discovered it. He was very much afraid he knew who.

"Why would he come back?" Nolan interrupted Nick's thoughts. "What's your theory?"

The question was probably rhetorical, but Nick told them about Horace's collection of movie memorabilia, pointing to a gruesome portrait on the opposite wall. The painting was of a martyred saint holding his own head and, from the look of things, asking to speak to upper management. The officers did not look impressed.

"I don't know what, if anything, this stuff is worth, but I do know a lot of this junk is the kind that appeals to adolescent males. And half the fun would be in liberating it."

"Speaking from personal experience?" Bruce asked dryly.

Nick shrugged. "I was a kid once. Sure."

"Okay, well, thanks for your help," Nolan said. "We'll let you know if we need more from you."

Diiis-missed! Nick had been afraid of that. There were just too many weird things about this case for the uniforms to rubber-stamp it accidental death. One of those things being Horace's celebrity status. Another thing being his well-known crank status.

Nick headed downstairs and found that the coroner's team had arrived—on foot—along with more cops who were busily securing the scene. He made his way out to the terrace, where he could see Ned Duke and the Savitri girl having a cozy cup of coffee together amid the piles of autumn leaves.

"Good morning! The power's back on," Ami greeted him. "Would you like some coffee?"

"If it's no trouble, I would."

"No trouble." She jumped up and vanished through the segmented glass door.

Nick turned his attention on Duke, but was interrupted by Enzo hurrying up the steps from the courtyard.

"What's going on?" Enzo demanded. He sounded out of breath, as though he'd been running. "The place is crawling with cops. What's happened? What did they find?"

Nick filled Enzo and Duke in on the events of the morning. Duke looked ready to faint by the time he finished.

"He *slipped*? You're sure that's what happened?"

"I can't be sure, no. But I didn't see anything to indicate violence."

He glanced at Enzo, who seemed to have been struck dumb.

"No, I mean... Right." Duke drummed his fingers on the iron tabletop. "How would he even get in?"

"How is the alligator getting in?" Nick asked. "Maybe they both came in the same way."

Enzo came back to life. "This doesn't have anything to do with Wally!" he burst out.

Nick eyed him curiously. "I didn't say it did."

Further discussion was interrupted as Ami returned, carrying a metal coffee carafe and another mug. She was pale, her eyes wide with alarm. "There are police officers and people from the coroner's office inside. Nobody will say what's happened." She was looking straight at Nick. "Has someone *died*? Who?"

Enzo turned without a word, lumbering down the steps and disappearing into the courtyard.

"Enzo?" Ami watched him go, her expression bewildered.

"He's worried about them taking Wally," Duke said.

Ami's expression altered. She exchanged looks with Duke.

Nick was about to reassure her that the victim was not a hotel resident, when the glass door opened and Officer Bruce stepped outside. The expression on his ruddy doll's face did not bode well for a happy Halloween at Angel's Rest.

"There you are, Reno. Your client is refusing to speak to us."

Nick groaned inwardly. He said, "You want me to—"

"Nope," Bruce said with sour satisfaction. "We've already called it as a suspicious death. It's going to be up to the detective bureau to decide what happens next."

Ami gasped. "You mean it could be murder?"

"A suspicious death…" Duke repeated numbly.

"Thanks for letting me know," Nick said. He was wondering where Perry was in all this drama. He needed to let him know what was going down on his end, but he didn't dare leave the storm's epicenter yet.

"Whatever Daly is paying, it's not enough," Bruce commented. "I'd find another client if I were you." And on that cheery note, he departed.

Nick had just finished his coffee and was recounting an abbreviated version of his adventures for the third time when he, Duke, and Ami were joined on the terrace by the Winthrop woman and the rainbow-haired psychic.

"What on earth is going on?" Winthrop demanded. "There are policemen everywhere. Where's Horace?"

"Death has claimed another victim at Angel's Rest," announced Gilda, dragging a heavy iron chair across the bricks. The scrape and bump of the chair sort of lessened the portentousness of her pronouncement.

Nick inquired, "What was your first clue? The coroner's van parked in the drive?"

Gilda glared at him. "I can't see the drive from my room." She plopped down in the chair.

Ami, meanwhile, was reassuring Wynne Winthrop that nothing had happened to Horace; that the victim had been one of Horace's skeleton-clad harassers.

"Thank God for that at least," Wynne murmured, and she seemed sincere.

Nick studied her curiously. Having been married to a woman who did not take kindly to slights to her ego, he'd had some questions ever since Horace's midnight revelations.

In Nick's experience, friendships between men and women were always dicey. Horace's bisexuality and tendency to turn to Wynne when things weren't going well between him and Troy would have complicated that relationship. It wouldn't be surprising if Wynne had some deeply buried resentments—or maybe some not-so-deeply-buried resentments.

"There is a dark energy at Angel's Rest," Gilda said. "A dark presence."

"It's called lousy lighting, darling." Wynne took a cigarette and lighter out of a small red leather bag. She lit the cigarette, tilted her head back, and blew a stream of smoke into the chilly air like a whale expelling air through a blowhole. "Mice have dined on the wiring in this place for decades."

"When was the last time the building passed a safety inspection?" Nick asked.

The others laughed—which was kind of what he'd figured.

"Does Angel's Rest have any secret passages?" Nick did not like secret passages.

"They wouldn't be secret, then, would they?" Gilda retorted.

"It's not likely." Duke had been quiet for so long, Nick had almost forgotten he was still present. "This used to be a hotel. It was never a home."

"It's still not a home," Ami said.

Wynne gave them a long look. "Nothing's holding you prisoner here. You can always leave."

Ami turned scarlet.

You can check out anytime you like, but… What was the rest of the line from that Eagles' song?

Duke said, "Some of us are on a fixed income."

"Darling, that's pure luxury for those who have to rely on residuals and royalties." Wynne added, "Which would be you, wouldn't it? Aren't you living on your writing?"

"Well, yes," Duke said. "But Ami isn't."

Wynne smiled a little maliciously. "Living on your writing? No, not yet."

Ami turned red again—and Duke just about matched her shade.

As interesting as Nick found their group dynamic, he wanted to check in with Perry, who probably needed a break from Horace about now.

He excused himself and went back inside, where he was stopped by a plainclothes cop who introduced himself as Detective Camarillo.

Camarillo was tall, dark, and ridiculously handsome. He looked like the traditional Latin lover in old films, or maybe a modern guy with a slew of Grammys to his name. He wore a suit no cop should have been able to afford, and smelled like Old Madrid and new money.

His partner, Detective Marin, was a stocky, pugnacious-looking blonde in sensible shoes and a suit from Sears, which Nick knew because he owned the same suit.

As Camarillo briskly took Nick through the whys and wherefores, it became clear to Nick that Camarillo did not like PIs in general or Nick in particular, but then Nick mentioned working for the Tristar Group. Suddenly he had discovered the secret handshake.

Camarillo stopped eyeing him with that sarcastic little smile, put down his pen, and looked at Marin, who shrugged like, *How was I supposed to know?* Camarillo turned back to Nick. "You work for Rick and Roscoe?"

"That's right. Roscoe and I were in the SEALs together." Nick rarely pulled the SEALs card, but he had been feeling like he needed an edge with Camarillo, and this looked like it.

"You're *that* Nick Reno?"

"Well, yeah," Nick admitted, now self-conscious.

It turned out Roscoe, Rick, and Camarillo had grown up on the streets of Los Angeles. Tristar Group was the only private-investigations firm Camarillo could tolerate—besides which, the guy who had saved Roscoe Jones' life in Afghanistan was a great guy in Camarillo's book.

"Maybe we could get back to the case?" Marin suggested once the social niceties were out of the way.

"Sure, sure," Camarillo said. "So what do you think, Nick? Was it an accident, or are we looking at homicide?"

His smile was wide and charming, his eyes dark and guileless, and Nick knew whatever he said, Camarillo was going to take it with a grain of salt and make his own mind up. Nick revised his original opinion. He began to like the guy a lot.

"I think it's an accident. But there's something weird about this setup. I can't put my finger on it, but something's not right."

"Instinct," Camarillo agreed. "You've got it. I've got it. Marin took one look at this place and said *hinky*. She's never wrong."

Marin sighed.

"So, I'm not disbelieving you," Camarillo said. "I think everything points to an accident. But we've got to be thorough. Your client had a history with the victim."

"I understand," Nick said. He did.

"Believe me, I'm no bleeding heart. A man's home is his castle. In Daly's case, literally a castle. I think this punk got what he deserved. Terrorizing old folks? Not okay. But we also can't have senior citizens laying traps for juvenile delinquents."

Nick nodded.

Camarillo seemed to commune silently with Marin.

He offered Nick another of those gleaming I-just-won-my-twelfth-Grammy smiles. "Marin just had a great idea. Why don't we do this, maybe kill two birds with one stone? Why don't you sit in on our interviews? You've had a day to observe these people. Your insights could be useful. What do you think?"

"That would be beyond great," Nick admitted.

"That's what I think," Camarillo said—and winked.

CHAPTER ELEVEN

"**Y**ou told Nick you destroyed these letters." Perry looked up from the box of yellowed envelopes Horace had set before him on the dining-room table.

It had been a very long morning.

Perry had barely managed to get Horace back to his apartment before the police arrived to examine the body in the hall, and he still wasn't one hundred percent convinced he'd made the right call. Once Horace had been sure the dead man wasn't Troy, he had been almost gleeful that one of the "assassins" was dead. But that bloodthirsty good cheer gave way to anxiety about what his enemies would attempt next in retaliation. For the first time Perry had felt a flicker of sympathy for the disagreeable Nevins in their thankless role of Horace's only kin.

Then the police had knocked on the door and requested a word with Horace, and Horace had referred them—through Perry—to speak to his lawyer.

That had gone over about as well as one would expect.

It was just a matter of time before the law was back with reinforcements, but Horace seemed oblivious to his peril. Instead, he had ranted about everything from his previously mentioned lawyer to the difficulty of finding a sweetened cereal called French Toast Crunch on grocery-store shelves.

Eventually, he had disappeared into his bedroom and at last returned with a black-and-gray wig box full of letters.

Now Horace gazed back at Perry defiantly. "Yes."

"*Why?* How can he help if you won't give him all the facts?"

"These are not facts. These are…personal."

"But Mr. Daly—"

"Horace, lovey."

"Horace—" Perry swallowed the rest of it and shook his head. Arguing with Horace was what his mother used to call "an exercise in futility." He picked up the first envelope. A felt pen had been used to print the thick block-style characters of Horace's address. Despite the fact that the writing was print script, they did have a certain individual style. The tiny letters were all uppercase and pressed closely up against each other.

"Do you recognize the writing on the envelope?" Perry asked.

"Yes. It's Troy's."

"Do you have something with Troy's writing that I could compare this to?"

Without a word, Horace opened a cabinet drawer and handed over a battered script. There were notations all over it, and the notations did look similar to the print writing on the envelope. To Perry, at least, but he was no handwriting expert. The tops of the *T*s and crossbar of the *H*s certainly looked identical.

Perry laid the script aside and studied the envelope again. There was a cancelled stamp on the envelope, and the postmark indicated the letter had been mailed from Hollywood in 2013.

According to Nick, all mail was now sent to designated mail-processing stations for sorting and distribution to delivery post offices. Had that been true five years ago? If so, the postmark would indicate the local post office the mail had been sent from.

Perry opened the first letter.

The note was handwritten, and the writing seemed to match that of the envelope.

I have not forgotten. This will not be over until you are dead.

Not a specific threat, but definitely sinister.

No signature. Not even a *Yours truly, Mr. X.*

The next letter was shorter and more to the point.

You will die a horrible death. SOON.

And on it went.

I'm watching you.

You don't know who I am, but I never forget you.

I like planning your death.

Not particularly imaginative, in all honesty. In fact, they were a bit slogan-ish, kind of like evil taglines. *Taste the Rainbow! Just Do It! Die, Witch, Die!* Not that they wouldn't be frightening to receive. They would. Not least because, regardless of the lack of creativity, normal people didn't operate like this. This was the work of a disturbed mind.

Perry went through the next letters. More of the same.

As he shuffled through the stack, he noticed that the writing on a couple of the later envelopes was slightly different. The script wasn't quite so cramped, and there were a few lowercase letters in the address.

The content of the letters changed too. At first, they were very brief: a single hateful handwritten line. But about three years in, the letters grew much longer—they became full on diatribes—and they were typewritten.

Why? What did that change signify?

You have spent your whole life using people and discarding them. There is no one more selfish and cowardly than you. I used to think maybe you would learn from your mistakes and change, but I see now how foolish that was. You will never change, and you deserve everything that is going to happen to you. When my knife slides between your scrawny ribs, I will have to scrape and scrape to find your miserable, miserly heart. I will stab you and stab you, and there will be nothing but a black hole.

Perry felt his hair standing straight up.

There was a lot of that kind of thing.

It seemed clear that as the years passed, the author of the letters grew more and more angry. The part that didn't seem to jibe was the decision to start typing them. Using a typewriter seemed less personal. And yet the content of the letters was very personal, very emotional.

What did it all mean? Perry couldn't decide. Maybe the switch to a typewriter had been fueled by a practical consideration? Like the writer had arthritis. After all, Troy would be at least in his seventies by now. Or maybe as the letters grew more blatantly threatening (and illegal), a typewriter had seemed to offer more disguise than block print?

Or maybe someone was faking Troy's writing and had found it too difficult to fake entire pages?

Midway toward the bottom of the pile, he picked up an envelope, and his heart seemed to drop a few ribs down his chest.

There was no stamp.

No cancellation mark to indicate there had ever been a stamp.

This letter had not gone through any post office. It been hand-delivered.

Perry checked the rest of the way through the pile.

Only one letter was missing a stamp. Only one letter had been hand-delivered.

But when he checked the typewritten letter inside, the contents were *exactly* like all the others.

Meaning?

Meaning that the same person had authored all the letters, but on one occasion, this person had decided—or circumstances had required them—to hand-deliver their hate mail.

"How do you get your mail?" Perry asked.

Horace looked confused. "As anyone does."

"No, I mean, does the mail carrier leave it in a box and someone at Angel's Rest walks down to get it? Or does the mail carrier deliver right to the hotel?"

"They used to deliver, but now there's a box at the end of the road where we have to go pick it up. Wynne usually walks down to get it."

Wynne. Oh no. But it made sense. Horace had admitted the night before that Wynne had reason to feel used and discarded. And—although this was probably sexist—the tone of the letters, or at least the vocabulary and grammar, felt vaguely feminine in a way Perry couldn't quite define.

Wynne had motive and opportunity. As far as means, well, how hard was it to get hold of a typewriter?

Come to think of it, these days? Maybe more difficult than he knew.

Wait. Was she still using a typewriter? Maybe she was using a computer with a printer now?

Perry shuffled through the letters again, but no. The most recent letters still seemed to be produced on a typewriter. The lower case *o* had started out partially filled in, and by the last letter it was almost a solid black dot.

So Wynne had faked Troy's handwriting, but as the years went by and the letters had gotten longer and longer, she had resorted to using a typewriter so as not to give herself away? She had even gotten a little less meticulous about the envelopes because, after all, if Horace hadn't caught on by then, there was a good chance he wasn't going to.

"What are you thinking?" Horace asked, snapping Perry out of his reflections.

"Are these in order, do you know?"

"Yes."

Perry nodded thoughtfully. He studied the envelopes that came before and after the unmarked envelope. "It looks to me like these three arrived last year. Does that seem right to you?"

"Yes. I think so."

"When Wynne picks the mail up, what does she do with it? Does she leave it somewhere for everyone to grab? Or does she actually distribute it?"

"She brings my mail to me. I have no idea what she does with everyone else's. Perhaps she leaves it for them in the dining room."

Perry was starting to feel a little sick. Bad enough to receive these vicious things from a stranger. But to come from someone Horace knew, someone he liked and trusted? That seemed truly terrible.

"What is it?" Horace asked, watching him.

Perry tried to decide how to answer. His "case" was pretty circumstantial. He wanted to talk to Nick before he said anything that might destroy a decades-old friendship. Besides, he might be wrong about the postmark thing. The stamp could have fallen off, and there might be other reasons why there wasn't a postmark.

While he was making his mind up, someone thumped on the door to Horace's suite, and he was saved from having to respond.

Horace went to answer the door.

With a knock that forceful, Perry had been expecting the police, but it was Enzo in the hall, looking wild-eyed. He pushed into the room. "The cops are poking around everywhere! They're going to find Wally!"

Horace began to fume. "How dare they? They have no right! The bastard didn't die in the swimming pool. Why are they poking into what doesn't concern them?"

Perry listened to this exchange uneasily. If the police were searching the hotel grounds, they must suspect the prowler's death was not an accident. Where the hell was Nick in all this? Why didn't he at least text Perry to let him know what was happening?

Enzo looked at Perry, but it was obvious he didn't see him. He said to Horace, "Goddamned busybodies. If they find Wally, they'll sure as hell contact Animal Control. You have to do something!"

"Oh, I shall! Believe me, I shall. By God, they'll *rue the day*!" Horace was puffed up with outrage, but then he seemed to deflate. He stared at Enzo. "It's just… I don't know what I *can* do," he said helplessly.

"Get your lawyer. File a restraining order. File a cease and desist. I don't know what it's called, but you have to get them to stop. Now."

"It doesn't work like that," Perry said. "If they think they have probable cause—"

Enzo threw him a baleful look and spoke to Horace. "Tell them you'll sue."

Horace looked guilty and apologetic. "But I can't afford to sue anyone. And no one ever wins suing the government."

"You don't pay unless you lose," Enzo, who clearly had not attended law school, assured him. "Anyway, it's not the government; it's Animal Control. They can't just come and take a man's pet. There has to be just cause."

And Animal Control had it. Starting with the illegality of keeping an alligator as a pet. But Perry kept quiet. He had not missed the hostility in Enzo's eyes. Enzo thought Perry and Nick were trespassing on his turf.

"Maybe they won't find Wally," Horace said.

"Hell yes, they'll find him. They're poking their noses into everything. Asking people questions about things that don't concern them. Duke's still mad about that goddamned cat. He'd just love to tell them about Wally."

Perry's phone dinged with a text from Nick.

Okay?

Not one to waste words, Nick. Perry rolled his eyes and texted back: Yes. Still w/Horace. Where r u?

Police

Well, that was cryptic. If Nick was able to text him, he wasn't under arrest or anything, so what did it mean?

He was distracted by the sudden and unexpected escalation of the argument between Horace and Enzo.

"I've done everything for you, Horace. I gave up my career, my *life* because you needed me. You owe me this!"

Whoa. Wait. What?

Was Enzo gay?

Horace was getting angry too. "And you were paid for it."

"Not for the last twenty years I wasn't."

"You've lived here rent free."

"If you can call it living!" Enzo cried.

Perry could practically see sparks shooting from Horace's red-rimmed eyes. "You didn't use to be so fussy. You could have left anytime you liked. I never asked you to give up your career. *What* career? You're too old to be a stunt man. You were too old twenty years ago. You didn't give it up for me."

All at once Enzo was ice-cold. "If Wally goes, *I* go," he said, heading for the door.

"Then *go*," Horace shouted.

Enzo went through the door, and Horace leaped after him to slam it shut with such force, the bloodied, guillotined wax head of a French noblewoman bounced off the top of the TV and fell face-first on the floor.

CHAPTER TWELVE

Detectives Camarillo and Marin took Nick's recommendation and began their interviews with Sissy and Jonah Nevin. Nick had no idea how reliable the information from Sissy and Jonah might be, he just knew there would be a lot of it. And he was right.

The Nevins were receiving in their bathrobes—Sissy, completely made up despite the early hour, wore a silver number that would have looked perfect on the set of *Lost in Space* (the original series), and Jonah wore a purple-and-blue smoking jacket. He was not a smoking-jacket kind of fellow, so the effect was more the-washing-machine-ate-my-bathrobe.

Sissy professed astonishment that the police were in the house—despite the view from her giant picture window of uniformed officers leaning over the fence surrounding the pool yard and pointing at the giant alligator swimming through the murky green water. The officers were shouting to each other and using their radios. Kind of hard to miss.

Jonah offered them orange juice, waffles, and a sickly smile. "Terrible thing. Terrible thing. We try not to associate with these people more than we have to. Horace is family, of course."

Camarillo graciously declined the offer of breakfast on behalf of himself and Marin, and took a seat on the green love seat—which immediately half swallowed him, though never had a man looked so dignified sinking into the furniture. Marin had shrewdly opted for the wooden chair by the antique sewing table, where Nick had sat the first time he met the Nevins. Nick chose to stand off to the side, where he had a perfect view of the Nevins but was not in their direct line of sight.

"I can't say I'm surprised," Sissy said in that breathy, girlish voice, once Camarillo had explained the situation. "Not that I'm blaming anyone, but people have been encouraging these fantasies of Horace's, and that just gets him more excited and worked up." She threw Nick a sorrowful look.

"Sadly, Bennie Regan, our victim, is as real as you are," Camarillo said.

"Oh, I don't doubt it!"

"Had you ever met Mr. Regan?"

"Not to our knowledge," Jonah said promptly. A little dog hoping for a big cookie.

Sissy, however, was not in quite such a hurry to end the visit. She bit her lip, looking reflective. "Regan is such a common name. Perhaps if you could describe him?"

"We can do better than that," Marin said in an unexpectedly melodious voice. She rose and showed the photo on her phone to Sissy and Jonah.

"Is that—? Is he—?" Jonah seemed to lose color.

"Yes," Marin said. "This is Mr. Regan, deceased."

Sissy was still studying the photo. She began thoughtfully, "You know, Father…" She stopped, flicked Camarillo an apologetic smile. "No. I'm sorry. I think he just has one of those faces. You'll ask Horace about him, of course."

"Of course," Camarillo said as Marin returned to her place by the window.

"Horace has a great fondness for young men." Sissy threw Nick a rueful look. "Mr. Reno's friend is currently a favorite of Horace's. It never lasts long, of course, and at least Mr. Foster seems like a kindhearted boy."

Nick raised his brows but did not bite.

"Walk me through last night," Camarillo invited.

Sissy and Jonah were eager to comply. They told Camarillo all about the strange dinner where Horace had announced he was hiring a private investigator, although he had no money to do anything so ridiculous. They critiqued the food, speculated on Ami Savitri's relationship with Ned Duke, castigated Gilda Storm as a sham and charlatan who encouraged Horace's delusions and paranoia, dismissed Wynne Winthrop as a washed-up has-been shamelessly pining for a man with unnatural desires for other men young enough to be his grandchildren, shook their heads over Enzo Juri, who was to be commended for his loyalty to Horace and the work he did with disadvantaged youths, but who was, after all, a secret drinker and owned an illegal exotic animal that posed a deadly threat to everyone on the property—not to mention all the cats and dogs in Laurel Canyon.

Marin and Camarillo took notes and exchanged frequent glances.

Nor did the revelations stop there. If Ned Duke had ever successfully published anything, it was news to them. Ami Savitri worked as a Sous Chef at NBC Universal and made pretty good money for a woman her age, so why was she living in a wreck like Angel's Rest, *hmmmmm*? Wynne Winthrop had been married four times, and her last husband had died under mysterious circumstances and left her a bundle—

"What happened after you got a headache and left the dinner table?" Camarillo interrupted, doggedly pursuing his trail no matter how many times the Nevins jumped in creeks or ran across rocks.

Sissy's cheeks grew pink. "Father and I came back here and tried to decide what we should do. We're Horace's only living family, after all, and if he's going off the rails again, it's up to us to see people don't take advantage of him." She did not look at Nick that time.

"If you believe your cousin is making up these threats, how do you explain the gang that attacked him Friday afternoon and Bennie Regan being found dead on the third floor of this hotel?" Camarillo questioned.

Sissy folded her hands and pressed her lips together. Her expression grew saint-like. Jonah, watching her, said, "I think we should tell them, Mother. For his own sake."

"Thinking is not proof," Sissy said.

Camarillo said, "We'll bear that in mind. What is it you believe?"

"I believe Horace has hired these young thugs. I believe they are extras in his homemade movie."

"His homemade movie?"

"Horace can no longer tell the difference between reality and fantasy. That's very obvious. At first, I assumed he was making everything up. The threats, the attacks on his life—for heaven's sake, he once claimed that someone had loosened the headboard of his bed so that it would fall on him! But if he's not making these latest incidents up, and I must admit that seems to be the case, then Horace himself must have arranged for these attacks. You'll notice they always occur when someone is there to save him."

"What's on the fourth floor?" Nick cut in.

Sissy looked momentarily confused. "A lot of old junk, I suppose. I haven't been up there in years."

After finding Regan's body, Nick had gone all the way up to the top floor to make sure no other intruders were in the building. He had not found anyone else, but on the fourth and fifth levels he had discovered a cache of costumes as well as a small hoard of movie props and set decorations.

In addition to all the movie memorabilia, there was a lot of antique furniture being stored up there.

So while Horace might be cash poor, he did have assets that could be readily liquidated for cash. It was more than possible he could raise the dough to hire some punks to pretend to threaten him.

The problem was, Horace was a collector, and collectors did not like to part with their collections.

Perhaps anticipating where Nick was going with his line of inquiry, Camarillo asked, "Mr. Daly is an older gentleman. Once he's gone, who inherits all this?"

Nick kept his face blank.

Sissy and Jonah looked at each other.

"I have no idea," Sissy said. "Horace is always changing his will." She glanced at Nick. "I wouldn't be surprised if this week your wide-eyed young friend is Horace's so-called heir." She gave a ladylike snort.

After interviewing the Nevins, Camarillo and Marin moved on to Gilda Storm, who spent thirty minutes babbling about the dark presence haunting Angel's Rest, two minutes complaining that the radiator in her apartment didn't work, and one final minute on the likelihood of Wally the Alligator killing someone if the law didn't do something.

"Animal Control has been notified," Camarillo reassured her.

Next up was Ami Savitri, who offered them raspberry turnovers and the information that she liked to bake when she was stressed.

To which Marin replied, "Your cookie jar must never be empty in this place."

Amy made a face. "It wasn't so bad at first. It was even kind of fun. The rent was amazing, and everyone seemed quirky and colorful. I loved Horace's movies when I was a kid. But lately, yeah, it's been weird."

She was a polite and conscientious witness. She professed to have no knowledge of the dead man and admitted that until the previous evening, she too had believed Horace was making up the threatening letters and mysterious accidents-that-weren't-accidents.

"I figured he was bored and lonely," she said and winced. "I feel terrible now. Imagine something like that going on, and no one believes you."

As for her movements on the night in question, after dinner she and Ned had shared a glass of wine in the old library, which was kind of their special hangout—no one else ever went into the east wing—and then they sneaked back to their rooms and said good night.

Camarillo grinned charmingly, and said, "Did you say good night in your room or Mr. Duke's?"

Ami blushed. "Oh, we're not—that is, we do sometimes, but not last night. Ned wanted to work, and he has to obey the muse when she calls. I guess."

Hoo-boy, Nick thought. She really liked Duke if she could swallow that line of guff whole.

It was obvious to Nick that not only was Savitri not part of any sinister conspiracy—thanks to being the kind of person who minded her own business—she was not going to have a lot of useful observations to share. Say what you would about the Nevins, they had been a fount of information.

Camarillo and Marin closed their notebooks and rose.

On impulse, Nick said, "Why do you think that alligator keeps trying to get into your rooms?"

He didn't expect her to have an answer, so the look of guilt that flooded her face came as a surprise.

"He's *hungry*," she said. "Enzo can't afford to feed him enough anymore. Do you know how much an alligator that size eats? I used to bring him leftovers and scraps from where I work at the studio, but it backfired. Wally started associating me with food. I don't know how he keeps getting out, but when he's loose, he comes straight for me."

"He won't be getting loose again," Camarillo promised. "Animal Control will take care of that."

She looked horrified. "They're not going to kill him, are they?"

Camarillo and Marin were amused. "No. No, of course not. He'll go to the LA Zoo most likely."

"That's sad. He may not know he's an alligator," Ami said.

"Trust me," Nick said. "He knows he's an alligator."

Camarillo was still chuckling about that when they stepped into the hall.

"An alligator always knows it's an alligator," he misquoted. "Is that your philosophy, or did you get it off *Animal Planet*?"

"It's my observation," Nick said, and Camarillo laughed again.

Marin stepped aside to make a phone call, and Nick accompanied Camarillo to Ned Duke's rooms. He felt a little guilty about leaving Perry trapped babysitting Horace for so long, but the opportunity to sit in on these interviews could not be missed.

And, after all, coming here this weekend had been Perry's idea.

Ned Duke was nervous.

That was obvious from the minute he opened his door. He was pale, he was sweaty, and he was talking too much.

"What a terrible thing to happen. He probably had a heart condition. Maybe. Maybe the place *is* haunted. Why would he be up there anyway? Maybe that accident ended up saving Horace's life. Because he couldn't have been up to any good."

He did not ask them to sit down.

"I hope this won't take long. I'm in the middle of a very tricky scene. Once you lose your train of thought, it's hell trying to get it back. I don't mean to be rude; it's just I don't *know* anything and I have this deadline."

It couldn't have been clearer if he'd run up a Jolly Roger. Granted, Duke would make one skittish pirate.

Nick was pleased to see that Camarillo picked up the same signals. The tone of the interview was different right from the start. Gone was the charming smile and approachable attitude. Camarillo glanced at the laptop sitting on the coffee table in front of the leather sofa. "Is this an article or a book you're working on, sir?"

"A b—an article, but I am also working on a book."

"I see. What's the article about?"

Duke proceeded to lie—badly—about writing an article on the top ten open source productivity tools, while Nick surveyed what he could see of the apartment. It was immediately obvious that Duke's quarters were more comfortably furnished than anyone else's they'd interviewed so far.

In addition to the leather sofa, he had a huge wooden rustic-design entertainment center with a flat-screen TV and a high-end stereo system. He had a large ivory area rug plush enough to sleep on. He had a seven-piece dining set and framed watercolors on the walls. In short, he was not enduring the hand-to-mouth existence of most of his neighbors. Yet supposedly he was eking his living at one of the most precarious professions out there. As Nick well knew from living with a guy eking his living from one of the others.

That wasn't the only red flag. A tower of soda crates—some so old they looked hand-painted—leaned against the wall next to the entertainment center. Nick was not an expert in antiques, but Perry cared about such things, and it was because of Perry's gloating triumph at scoring a beat-up soda crate from the 1940s that Nick knew those boxes went for up to two hundred dollars each.

Same with that little crowd of dusty mason jars on the dining-room table. Depending on a number of variables, those could go from twenty to one thousand dollars apiece.

And vintage marbles? Very collectible. A single marble from the 1800s could go for one hundred dollars or more on eBay.

Camarillo had finished grilling Duke about his writing, and invited him to share his movements on the previous evening.

Duke cleared his throat and glanced nervously at Nick. "Well, after the incident with the prowler, we all went inside and tried to convince Horace to phone the police. But he wouldn't. I'm not sure why, because there were plenty of witnesses, so no one could accuse him of making it all up this time."

"Go on," Camarillo said.

"Mr. Reno can vouch for all that."

Nick was amused. "Sure."

"All that is not the part I'm interested in," Camarillo said crisply. "What happened after dinner?"

Duke went paler still. "After dinner? After dinner, Ami— that's the young woman across the hall—"

"We know who Ami is," Camarillo said.

"Oh. Right. Well, Ami and I were together."

Camarillo smiled like a cheerful tiger. "All night?"

"Uh, well, y—I mean, you know. A lady's reputation." Duke cleared his throat again.

Camarillo said to Nick, "Did we just time-travel back to the 1800s when I wasn't looking?"

"Maybe," Nick said. "Going by some of the antiques I see lying around here."

Duke groaned, collapsed on the sofa, and put his face in his hands. "All right, all right! I admit it. I was up there. It was me. But it was an *accident*. My God, how do you think I feel? I'm sick over it. I would never— *I thought I got them all!*"

"What the hell are you talking about?" Camarillo inquired.

"He lost his marbles," Nick said. He couldn't resist it. But it really wasn't a joking matter. "Mr. Duke here has been supplementing his writing income by stealing from his landlord." He said to Duke, "What do you do, sell everything on eBay?"

"Etsy," moaned Duke. "It's a more targeted market, and the seller fees are lower."

Camarillo said, "What the hell?"

"I've been up on the top floors," Nick said. "I think they're primarily being used to store Horace's collections and a bunch of the hotel's old furniture."

Face still in his hands, Duke nodded.

"There's a lot of junk up there. Rotting mattresses and broken furniture. But there's valuable stuff too. Some of it is too big to be moved without getting caught, but there are plenty of small, highly collectible items that could be easily lifted with no one the wiser."

Duke raised his head. "It's true. Okay? I'm not denying it. Horace doesn't care about that stuff. He probably doesn't even remember most of it is still there. What use is it, leaving it to rot? What happened last night was *an accident*. I was carrying a paper bag of marbles, and the bag tore. A few of the marbles fell out. I thought I got them all. I was going to go back when it was daylight to make sure, but…"

Nick said, "But in the meantime, one of Horace's harassers was snooping around the house—who knows, maybe with the same idea of pocketing a few items to keep as souvenirs or maybe even to pawn?—and he slipped on one of the marbles and fell down the staircase."

"We don't know that for sure," Camarillo said. "We still have to get the ME's report. For all we—"

"We do know," Marin interrupted. She had slipped inside the front door while Nick was talking. She held up her cell phone. "I just got off the phone with the ME. Preliminary findings are consistent with an accidental fall down a wooden staircase."

CHAPTER THIRTEEN

"Of course I'm pressing charges!" Horace said when he was informed of Ned Duke's sideline business. "Right after I throw him out. I won't have that thief under my roof another night."

"He won't be under your roof tonight," Detective Camarillo said. "Tonight he'll be in jail on a slew of charges, including involuntary manslaughter."

Camarillo looked like he had stepped out of a magazine—possibly *POLICE Magazine.* He was pleasant and patient with Horace, and showed no sign that he thought Horace was a nut or making up stories to get attention. His partner, Detective Marin, had a nice smile and, unless Perry was losing his eye, was hiding a baby bump beneath that men's suit jacket. She didn't so much as blink at the two skeletons sitting at Horace's dining table.

"The thing is," said Nick, who was sitting next to Perry on the velvet sofa, "Duke isn't the one sending you hate mail."

"It *must* be Duke," Horace objected. "He and his confederates were trying to scare me into abandoning Angel's Rest so they could swoop in and steal all my treasures."

Camarillo said, "We have to agree with Mr. Reno, sir. We don't believe Duke was working with anyone. His story is credible."

Horace stubbornly shook his head—and kept shaking it.

"Duke doesn't have a motive," Nick said. "The scenario you're describing makes no sense."

"Uh, Nick..." Perry said.

Nick qualified, "What I mean is, the last thing Duke wanted or needed was any kind of investigation, however informal, taking place at Angel's Rest. He did not want the police paying you a call, let alone a PI coming to stay the weekend. From his point of view, those letters brought exactly the wrong kind of attention. Besides which, he doesn't seem to have any particular grudge against you."

"He likes the girl," Camarillo said, and Marin nodded. "He wouldn't do anything to harm her. We have a theory—and Mr. Reno shares it—that whoever was letting that alligator out of its pen and into the hotel needed a distraction."

Was that the answer? Using an alligator as a distraction seemed kind of a bad idea to Perry. True, it would be an effective way to divert attention. But it would also be guaranteed to put everyone in the hotel on high alert. Wouldn't someone trying to sneak in prefer to do it quietly and unobtrusively? Wouldn't that offer a better chance of success? Especially in the middle of the night when there was a good chance everyone was asleep and not paying attention anyway.

But if Wally was not being used as a distraction, why *was* he being let loose?

"Then who *is* to blame?" Horace demanded.

Marin said, "We'd like to show you a photo of the young man who died here last night—"

Horace waved her off. "I don't know him. I don't recognize him."

Awkward—given that Marin had not yet shown Horace the photo. Perry was trying to come up with a good excuse for having allowed Horace to visit the possible crime scene, when rescue came in the form of Nick's ringing cell phone.

Nick pulled his phone out and checked it. He rose, saying, "I have to take this." He stepped into the hall, closing the door behind him.

"This is a photo of Bennie Regan." Marin offered the photo on her phone, apparently putting Horace's response down to general crotchetiness.

Horace took her phone and turned it sideways and upside down. Perry wondered if he was pulling their leg, but he said finally, "I'm not sure. Now that I have a good look at him."

"You're not sure of what?" Camarillo asked.

"Maybe he does look familiar."

Camarillo's gaze narrowed. "You think you recognize him?"

Horace shrugged. "It's hard to say. He may have been one of Enzo's boys."

"Enzo's boys?"

"Enzo Juri. He used to be my bodyguard. He helps out at the YMCA. Teaches boys to box. Sometimes he'd bring them here to work around the place for a few dollars."

Camarillo and Marin held a quick conference.

"We haven't interviewed Juri yet," Marin said.

"It makes sense," Camarillo said. "The kid did some work, noticed there were items lying around that could be sold or pawned—kind of the same idea Duke had."

The door opened, and Nick beckoned to Perry.

Perry joined him out in the hall. Nick was apologetic.

"Roscoe just called. I've got to go in to work. Grab your stuff, and I'll drop you off at home first."

Perry's disappointment gave way to surprise. "I can't leave."

Nick frowned. "Of course you can. Of course you will. You can't stay here."

"Of course I can. Of course I will," Perry shot right back. "I gave my word."

"Perry, this isn't— The situation here is still unresolved. I don't think Regan has been sending Horace love notes for the last five years. He'd have had to start when he was about fourteen."

Perry had already drawn the same conclusion. "I think I know who's sending the letters—and why."

"Who?"

"Wynne." Perry quickly filled Nick in on his morning with Horace and the reasoning behind the deductions he'd made reading through the letters.

Nick heard him out in silence. "Not bad," he admitted when Perry was finished. "In fact, as circumstantial cases go, that's just about airtight. But are you sure you want to get in the middle of that?"

"No. I don't. I'm not sure what I'm going to do. I could try talking to her—"

Nick said quickly, "I don't like that idea."

Perry gave him a look of exasperation. "I think I can probably hold my own against a seventy-year-old woman."

"That's not what I mean. I *mean*, it's not going to be pleasant, and I don't think you want to be stuck here trying to mediate between the two of them. The Savitri girl has gone to try to bail out Duke, and God only knows what's going on with Enzo. Plus, it's Halloween. You don't want to be here on Halloween."

"I wasn't actually planning on trick-or-treating," Perry said.

It was Nick's turn to be exasperated. "I know that. I'm not suggesting you're a child or not strong enough to handle the situation. I'm just saying, why would you *want* to? This isn't your problem."

"Because I promised, Nick. I promised we'd stay through Halloween."

"But the case is solved."

"It's *not* solved. Not entirely. You just said yourself the situation was unresolved." Perry wasn't quite sure why he was getting irritated with Nick—probably a lot of it was the disappointment of their weekend together being cut short. Not that he didn't understand, but it was still a letdown.

"It's solved enough for now," Nick snapped, also getting irritated. "It's solved enough for tonight."

"I'm not leaving with you," Perry said flatly. "I can't leave until Monday morning."

Nick's face tightened. He opened his mouth to say something he immediately thought better of. He scowled and said instead, "All right. If that's your decision, I'll pick you up tomorrow morning. You can text me when you're ready to go."

Perry's heart sank. He and Nick never argued about anything. Not even little silly things. They just didn't. He hated feeling he was behaving unreasonably, or that Nick was angry with him, but he *had* given his word. Horace didn't know the source of the letters yet, and he was still frightened.

Perry nodded, and Nick eyed him unsmilingly. "Okay. Well. I'll talk to you later."

"Talk to you later," Perry clipped out because his throat had closed unexpectedly. He hesitated—he did not want to say goodbye on these terms—but Nick looked unbending, and it was hard to make the move to kiss someone who looked so… stony. After all, Nick was not making any move to kiss *him*.

Perry turned and went back inside Horace's apartment.

After speaking with Horace, Detectives Camarillo and Marin interviewed Enzo. Perry knew that because Enzo came straight to Horace afterward and called Horace a horse's ass for believing that Enzo could ever have been part of a scheme to terrorize and defraud him.

"If you want to suspect someone," Enzo shouted, "maybe you should look at those leeches Sissy and Jonah. They hired Bennie and his friends to paint their apartment last summer."

Horace surprised Perry then, because instead of getting mad at Enzo, he cried and assured him he never believed it for one second. Which Perry was able to confirm. Camarillo and Marin had toyed with that scenario for a few minutes, and Horace had steadfastly refused to believe that Enzo would steal from him.

Enzo had seemed so enraged that morning, Perry had not expected a peaceful outcome, but by the time the two had argued it all out—and both had shed tears over Wally the Alligator being removed by Animal Control for relocation to a nice cozy zoo where he might actually get enough to eat—it looked like their friendship had been safely patched up.

The afternoon passed with no word from Nick.

Listening to Horace ramble on and on, Perry couldn't help thinking Nick could have been a little kinder about his decision to stay. It wasn't like Perry was having a great time at Angel's Rest. He was trying to do the right thing, which was something Nick usually approved of.

Anyway, virtue was supposed to be its own reward, so Perry did his best to enjoy the sight of Horace happily poring over his old photo albums while the bright afternoon slowly faded.

"This is when Sissy and Jonah moved in." Horace pointed to a Polaroid photo of a much slimmer Sissy and a more dapper Jonah sitting on the terrace of Angel's Rest. The Nevins were holding wineglasses and smiling. They looked like completely different people, but then they had been different people. They had been in their twenties back then. Angel's Rest looked different too. Not nearly as derelict and dilapidated.

"When was this taken?" Perry asked.

Horace made a face. "When I got out of the hospital. After Troy left."

"I didn't realize you were injured," Perry said. The way Sissy had told the story, Horace had stabbed Troy.

"I wasn't. It wasn't that kind of hospital," Horace said vaguely, still studying the photo as though looking for something hidden in the corners.

"Oh."

Horace looked up and smiled at Perry's expression. "I thought you knew the story?"

"Well, some of it."

"Ah. Well, I told you the important parts last night. Troy came home and found Wynne and me in bed together. We'd been smoking pot, of course, but I make no excuses. He tried to stab me, but ended up stabbing Wynne. Then I got the knife away from him and stabbed him."

Perry could not think of anything to say. Horace sounded almost breezy about it all.

"Not seriously, mind you. It was a flesh wound, but we were all quite upset, as you can imagine. The police were called, and the fact that we were doing drugs did not work in our favor. We were all arrested, and I was kicked off the movie I was doing at the time. Wynne went back East and did some Off-Off-Broadway. Troy was sentenced to a year, but was out in six months. I had a nervous breakdown and was hospitalized for a few months, and during that time, Sissy and Jonah moved in." Horace turned the page of the photo album.

"Did you ever see Troy after that?" Perry asked. Horace had said no the night before, but Perry wasn't sure if the story would be the same in the daylight.

"No." Horace's smile was twisted. "I shouldn't admit this, but I did try. I offered to forgive him. He still wouldn't come back."

Perry absorbed this for a moment or two. "You changed your mind about marrying Wynne?" That would probably have been the final straw for Wynne, the thing that had set her off on her years-long campaign of terror. Her bitterness must have festered and grown—

But Horace laughed. "Oh no! I'd have happily married her. I adore Wynne. And it would have solved the problem of Sissy and Jonah digging themselves in for all eternity on the pretext of looking after me. No, Wynne wouldn't have me after that. She said we were both safer sticking to friendship."

Perry could hear his theory about the authorship of the poison-pen letters crashing and burning. Not Wynne. And probably not Troy.

Both Wynne and Troy had passed on the opportunity of a future with Horace. While Perry was no expert on obsession, common sense indicated that obsessed people did not decline the chance to engage with the object of their obsession.

And another thing. Since when was obsession seasonal? Why did the letters start arriving every Halloween? That seemed weirdly calculated. Like Halloween was the scariest time of year, so that might be a good time to start up again? Or Halloween might provide some cover because a lot of loony things happened then? *Or...*

"What time of year was it when all that happened with Troy and Wynne?" Perry asked.

"What *time* of year?" Horace seemed puzzled.

"Right. Because you said last night Troy had returned from meeting with his coven. Was it—"

"Halloween," Horace said promptly, understanding. "It happened on Halloween night."

THE GHOST HAD AN EARLY CHECK-OUT   175

CHAPTER FOURTEEN

It was a relief when Perry's picture flashed up on Nick's cellphone screen.

Nick was on stakeout, sitting in the cramped confines of his car, watching the closed blinds in the window of Room 206 at—kid you not—Le Rendezvous Motel in Van Nuys and feeling like an absolute shit for busting Perry's balls about sticking it out at Angel's Rest.

Of course Perry was going to keep his promise to Horace. *Of course* that was the right thing to do.

It was just… From the—very likely—lead paint on the walls to the—possibly dangerous—crackpots who dwelled within, that was not a healthy space. Even minus the alligator, the sneak-thief tenant, and the sword-carrying, disgruntled former employees, that was not a place for someone like Perry. The air itself was unhealthy.

None of which excused Nick acting like a jerk.

And still, knowing all that—feeling all that—Nick could only rasp out a gruff, "Hey."

"*It's the Nevins*," Perry exclaimed. "Nick, it's the Nevins. It's *got* to be."

"What's the Nevins?" Nick asked cautiously. First and foremost was relief that Perry, as usual, was not holding a grudge. He did not sulk, he did not hold grudges, he was not spiteful. Nick had never known anyone as easy to get along with, which made him all the more impatient with his own behavior.

"The Nevins are writing those poison-pen letters to Horace. I *know* it."

"What makes you think so?"

"He's not dead," Perry said.

"I'm not following."

"They're not trying to kill him. If they wanted him dead, he'd be dead by now. They want him to have another break-down. They want him to be found crazy so that they can take over the property. The land this hotel is sitting on is worth millions. But Horace won't sell. Won't even consider it. If they killed him, they'd be the number-one suspects. Plus, Horace is always changing his will, so they can't even be sure they would inherit."

"Go on," Nick said.

"I think at first they were just biding their time, waiting for Horace to go off the deep end or die a natural death. But they've been waiting forty years, and Horace is still pretty healthy and, yes, he's eccentric, but he's not crazy."

"Debatable," Nick said, "but go on."

"I think they finally got tired of waiting, and for the last few years, they've been giving him a little push because Halloween is when it all happened."

"Perry, honey—" Nick stopped, startled at the sound of that word slipping so naturally off his tongue. He had never called anyone "honey" before. He had never been a guy for endearments. Heck, he didn't even use nicknames. But somewhere along the line, he had become a guy who used words like that. Somewhere along the line, Perry had gone from being his guy to being his honey.

Perry hadn't noticed and was still racing through his reasoning. "Horace is more fragile this time of year. He starts going through his scrapbooks and photo albums, and he starts remembering. That's why it always happens at Halloween. And I think this year everything is escalating because they're tired of waiting. I think Jonah unlocked the pool yard and left the hotel door open so that Wally could get in. I don't think it was intended as a distraction or anything like that. I think they deliberately let Wally out in hopes that something awful would happen or almost happen, and then the hotel would have to be shut down. The best thing that could happen for them is to get rid of everyone else, all the potential witnesses, and then focus on driving Horace over the edge."

"This is a lot of supposition," Nick said. But there was a crazy logic to it. And Perry was absolutely right about the value of the land Angel's Rest sat on. People had committed murder for a lot less. In this case, they didn't even have to commit murder. Just get poor old Horace locked away forever and have themselves appointed his trustees. Sissy had more than once offered the opinion that Horace was mentally unbalanced.

"It's the reason for those stupid skeleton costumes and why they didn't really make sense in the context of Horace's movies. Because they weren't the choice of an obsessed fan. They were the choice of someone who wanted Horace to talk about getting attacked by skeletons with swords. I'll bet you anything that Sissy and Jonah hit on the idea of using Bennie and his friends when they were working around the hotel for Enzo."

"Okay, slow down," Nick said. There was a hell of a lot to process in all that.

"And," Perry added grimly, "I bet Bennie got the idea all on his own to sneak in and see what he could steal because he was already familiar with the place."

Nick tried to remember if there had been any clue that Sissy recognized Bennie. And yes, she had sort of hemmed and hawed about whether she knew him. Which was smart in the event that Bennie was connected to Enzo—which was apparently what had happened.

"It's all separate, but it's all connected," Perry finished triumphantly.

"Listen to me," Nick said. "Have you shared this theory with Horace?"

"Not yet, no."

"Don't. Not tonight. Don't tell him tonight. And don't confront the Nevins on your own. Don't give any hint that you suspect what you suspect. We'll talk to them together tomorrow. Okay? And if it looks like your theory is correct—and you've already got me more than halfway convinced—I'll take this to Detective Camarillo. Fair enough?"

"Yes."

"Also"—Nick sucked in a long breath—"I apologize for being a jackass earlier."

Perry made a small amused sound. "Apology accepted."

"Of course you wouldn't go back on your word. And I shouldn't have pressured you to."

"You're just worried about me. I know." The cheerful confidence shook Nick. He couldn't stand the thought of doing anything to damage that.

"It's true. You're the most important thing in the world to me."

"It's the same for me," Perry said. "So be careful tonight. Don't get in the way of any jealous husbands or wives."

"I won't. And on that note, it might be a good idea if you stayed the night with Horace. Just to be on the safe side."

"I was thinking the same thing," Perry said, surprisingly. "I don't think the Nevins are killers, but they probably didn't start out as the kind of people who bullied and abused elders either."

The door of Room 206 opened.

"I'll see you tomorrow morning," Nick said, and clicked off.

* * * * *

Dinner was strained.

Enzo stayed in his room, mourning the loss of Wally. Ami arrived home and announced to the astonishment of everyone she was packing and would be moving in with Ned as soon as they could find a place together. Wynne was dining out with friends. Gilda was attending a Halloween séance. Maybe unsurprisingly, Horace was gloomy and preoccupied, picking at his food and drinking too much wine. Only the Nevins seemed eerily normal as they consumed the lion's share of the previous night's leftovers and chatted about the remarkable events of the day as if it had all happened to people on TV.

Knowing about them what he was sure he did, Perry found it difficult to make table talk, but it seemed the Nevins needed no one but each other to keep their little party going.

"Do you get trick-or-treaters?" Perry asked when there was finally a lull in the conversation.

"No," Horace said.

"Angel's Rest is too far for any child to walk to," Sissy said. "We've had the gardens vandalized a few times on Halloween night." She smiled at Jonah, who smiled back at her.

All at once Perry knew what they reminded him of. Vampires. He resolved to lock himself and Horace in for the night as soon as humanly possible.

But once dinner was finally over and they *were* locked in for the night, the hours dragged.

Horace continued to drink and grow more and more morose as he brooded about the past and his relationship with Troy, who he still believed was the one sending him those terrible letters.

Listening to him, Perry began to wonder uncomfortably if Horace actually *would* be relieved to learn Troy was not still obsessed with him—because Horace was clearly still obsessed with Troy.

It was pretty depressing. They seemed to have really loved each other at one time—they certainly looked very happy in all those photos in Horace's picture albums. It was sad to think how love could slowly, inexorably be chipped away at until nothing was left. A good reminder to make sure to pay attention to the details of his relationship with Nick. Not that he was worried. Nick was a detail-oriented guy.

By eleven o'clock, Perry was tired—he had not had much sleep the night before—and counting the minutes until Horace crashed. Not that he was looking forward to sleeping on the dusty couch under the glassy gaze of the creepy dolls, but anything was preferable to hearing another word about Troy.

Far from getting sleepy, as the hours passed, Horace seemed to grow more energized.

Maybe the word was manic?

Eventually, Horace hit on the idea of getting out a projector and watching old home movies.

"It's kind of late," Perry said doubtfully. He could think of nothing he would rather do less than watch Horace's home movies. Unless it was watch Horace's theatrically produced movies.

"I never sleep on Halloween," Horace said.

Which was when Perry learned there *was* something he'd rather do less than watch home movies, and that was go *find* the projector and reels of film.

"Enzo put them in the east tower," Horace said. "I told him I never wanted to see them again, so he stored them where I would never have to."

Wouldn't destroying the films have guaranteed never having to see them again? But okay, unsurprisingly, Horace had changed his mind about that—which Enzo had likely anticipated.

"Will I be able to find them easily?" Perry asked.

"Oh, you don't need to find them," Horace said in surprise. "I'll get Enzo to bring them down to us."

Perry glanced at the clock in the dining room. Even if dragging Enzo out of bed at nearly midnight to fetch and carry for Horace was normal procedure, he did not want to risk another blowup between Horace and his former bodyguard. Plus, Enzo was truly distraught over Wally's departure. It seemed needlessly unkind to intrude on that.

"It's okay. I'll go," Perry said. "Will I need keys or anything?"

"You don't want to be wandering around the place at midnight," Horace protested. "Believe me, I know what I'm talking about when I say it's damned spooky over in that wing at night. We'll just send Enzo."

Perry laughed. "No, it's fine. I'll do it." He added hopefully, "Unless you think maybe you might want to go to sleep?"

"No, I won't sleep." Horace was adamant.

Perry sighed. "Okay then. But you've got to promise to keep the door locked until I'm back. Don't open it to anyone but me. Promise?"

Horace put up his hand. "My word as an officer and a gentleman."

"Uh, okay. Well, I'm holding you to it," Perry said, and took the ring of keys Horace handed over.

"They're all the way over in the east tower," Horace said. "Did I tell you that already? I'm not sure if you should use the elevator on that side. It's not maintained like the one over here. The emergency lights should be on, though. It's the little stairway off the eighth floor."

"Okay, got it." Perry stepped into the gloomy hallway, waited until Horace turned all the locks, and then set off toward the elevator.

There were lights on when he reached the ground floor, but they were dim and mostly seemed to serve as the best method of casting macabre shadows against the walls and ceiling. It was deadly quiet. No lamps shone beneath any door all down the main hallway, so it looked like everyone who was home had gone to bed.

Perry crossed the empty, echoing marble foyer with its intimidating columns, cobwebbed light fixtures, and painted ceiling, annoyed with himself when he jumped at the unexpected sight of a zombie standing behind a large and very dead potted plant.

He reached a pair of interior French doors. They were supposed to be locked, but when he tried the door handle, they opened soundlessly. Someone was keeping those hinges well-oiled. Interesting.

Guided by the emergency lights, he went through another smaller lobby and past a gift shop that appeared to have been in the process of being turned into a museum—it was kind of unlikely the row of shrunken heads in the window had been part of the original display.

He passed the ornate antique elevator, which was chained off in any case, and walked on, uneasily conscious of how loud the whisper of his rubber soles sounded in the dusty silence.

Thankfully, Horace's gruesome movie props had not made it past the gift shop. This part of the hotel felt menacing enough without ghoulish embellishments. Although, frankly, Perry was impatient with himself for reacting so strongly to the atmosphere. Imagine Nick getting freaked out by a few spiderwebs and poor lighting? Ridiculous.

No question, it did feel weird to be moving around this part of the hotel alone at night, and instinctively he walked softly and stuck to the shadows, feeling—irrationally—that he was being watched.

He came to the large staircase, the twin of the one in the west wing, and started up. Each time a floorboard squeaked, he flinched. The sound seemed so loud. He reached the first landing and heard something scampering down the hall away from him. Rats, very likely.

Why had he agreed to this again?

He started up the next flight of stairs. On the fourth level, the lights were completely out, and he had to talk himself into not giving up and going back down. He got control of his nerves and felt his way up the bannister to the fifth floor, where the emergency lights were back on again. Even that bit of dim radiance cheered him considerably, and he took the next three flights at a decent clip, despite the fact that his chest was starting to feel tight and scratchy.

When he reached the eighth floor, he stared down the corridor of dusty carpet and shredded wallpaper. He could see the moon shining brightly through an oriel window at the end of the hall. To the left of the window was a narrow white door.

Perry's heart began to thump against his breastbone in something close to panic.

He did not want to walk down that hall.

He did not want to open that door.

He did not want to climb the stairs to that tower room.

Which was idiotic.

I-D-I-O-T-I-C.

This was not instinct. This was irrational fear. And he was allowing it to drown out his common sense.

"Snap out of it!" he murmured, and then threw an uneasy look over his shoulder. The inky nothingness of the stairwell below him made him feel slightly dizzy.

He would get the projector and a couple of reels of film, go back down, and count the hours until Nick arrived and they could talk to Horace about the Nevins together.

Perry forced himself to start down the hallway. It seemed a mile long before he reached the white door. He tried the handle. It was locked. He had to use the flashlight app on his phone to see where to insert the key. He turned the knob, and the door opened with a hideous screech of hinges.

He had to go up another four narrow steps and unlock a shorter, bullet-shaped door. The door stuck. He had to put his shoulder against it, and then it popped open with a higher-pitched screech than the previous set of hinges.

Despite the cold night air blowing through the broken windows, the smell was ghastly. A crazy mix of gasoline and chicken coop. The darkness was utter and absolute—and, to his stricken horror, alive.

CHAPTER FIFTEEN

Nick's cell phone rang as he was finishing up his report on Sheila Burks, now safely returned home for the evening to her ever-loving, PI-hiring husband.

He was hoping it might be Perry again, but the number that flashed up was not one he recognized.

"Reno."

"Reno, it's Denis Camarillo."

"Hey," Nick said, surprised. "What's up?"

"I went ahead and ran a background check on your communicating threats suspect. There's no record of Tom Ciesielski aka Troy Cavendish after 1979."

Nick couldn't quite read Camarillo's tone. "You mean no further criminal activity on his jacket?"

"I mean no record, period. He dropped off the map after he got out of jail. And by map, I mean any and all maps. He disappeared completely."

"Voluntarily?" Nick didn't expect Camarillo to have an answer. He was just thinking aloud, and *voluntarily* was the best-case scenario of the options that occurred to him.

"Your guess is as good as mine," Camarillo said. "But whoever is sending nastygrams to Daly, it's not his ex."

Nick suddenly had a very bad feeling in the pit of his stomach—and it had nothing to do with the burrito he'd had for lunch.

"Thanks, man. I owe you." He disconnected, threw the clipboard to the seat beside him, and turned the key in the ignition.

* * * * *

Birds.

The east tower had become an aviary for the ravens. Perry could see them silhouetted briefly against the moon as they swooped in and out through the tall broken windows.

Now that he knew what they were, he was struck by the almost magical beauty of the scene before him. It looked like something out of a fairy tale: the birds and the moon and the shards of broken glass glittering like ice scattered across the floor.

Beautiful or not, he did not think he should be breathing that air, and he buried his nose and mouth in the crook of his arm.

In the silvery light he could see bowl-shaped piles of straw and sticks on the floor. Nests.

He did not see a projector or cannisters of film. Frankly, he had thought from the first that this seemed an unlikely place to keep film or even film equipment, and he was glad Enzo had thought better of it—though it would have been nice to know before he spent twenty minutes wandering around the east wing of the hotel. Nice to know before he climbed eight fucking flights of stairs.

Was he missing something in the shadows? The tower room was not large, but there were plenty of shadows stretching like long fingers across the dirty floor. No. No projector. No round tins of film.

There was a bundle of old clothes against one wall—he'd missed that at first.

As Perry stared, the hair rose on the back of his neck.

He shook his head. Because no. *No, no, no.* That could not be.

All the while he was reassuring himself that no, that was not what he was thinking it was, he was walking toward it, picking his way through the large, bulky nests, careful not to step on those dull, greenish-blue-spotted eggs.

Perry reached the pile of clothes and knelt. For an instant he was relieved, because this was not a body or even a skeleton. For a second or two he thought he was looking at one of Horace's movie props. A mummy. The wisps of hair, the leathered skin, the broken teeth. Very lifelike.

Then he saw that the remaining rags of garment consisted of denim jeans and what had probably been a red or purple shirt. He saw too that the floorboards were visible through the head of the mummy.

His stomach lurched, his lungs seemed to close up, and he struggled to pull in enough air—and not be sick.

This dusty trinket box of a room, scraping the bottom of the clouds, had become Troy Cavendish's coffin. The dry California winters and blazing hot summers had done their work. The birds had helped. There was almost nothing left of him.

Perry felt for his inhaler, clicked, sucked.

Calm down. He can't hurt you. Just breathe.

A floorboard creaked. He looked toward the doorway, and his heart nearly stopped.

A black, burly shadow stood in the archway.

He must have made some sound of alarm because the figure shifted, then seemed to settle into place. Decision made.

A flashlight beam hit him squarely in the eyes.

"Who…is…it?" Perry asked. He thought he knew. He clicked his inhaler again.

"Why did you have to come here?" Enzo asked. "Why did you have to make yourself a part of it?"

"Why…did you…have to…kill him?" Perry got out.

"Because he wouldn't stop! Because he was making Horace crazy. They made each other crazy. I told him not to come back. He wouldn't listen. I *told* him."

"Horace…wanted him…back."

"Yes! He did. Because he's nuts. I had to protect him from himself. He'd have been right back in the loony bin if I'd let that go ahead."

Does he have a gun?

Keep him talking.

The crazy thing was Perry couldn't think of anything to ask. Terror seemed to have sped up his mental processes. He already knew why Enzo had been so terrified of the police hunting around the hotel. He knew why he had been upset that Horace had hired a private investigator. He even knew that when he took too long finding the projector, Horace had gone ahead and woken up Enzo—and when Enzo heard where Perry was going, he had raced to try and head him off. He knew that Enzo was going to try to kill him as soon as he ran out of questions.

"Why…didn't you…feed him…to alligator?" The inhaler was helping. It was a little easier to get his breath now. Or maybe that was the fight-or-flight response kicking in, because if he was going to survive, he would have to do one or both.

"I thought of it. Maybe I should have. I didn't want to have a man-eater on my hands, for Chrissake."

"Horace is going to…remember… he sent you after me," Perry said.

"I don't think so. And so what if he does? I didn't find you. Horace is used to people letting him down." Enzo shrugged. "You won't be the first who checked out early from this hotel."

All the while they were talking, the ravens continued to fly in and out, agitatedly circling the tower room in an attempt to protect their nests. Now one of them flew toward Enzo as he stood blocking the doorway.

Enzo gasped and swung at the bird with his flashlight. Something heavy hit the floor.

A gun? A knife?

Perry scrambled for the door. The only way out was through Enzo, but Enzo instinctively dived for his weapon, leaving just enough space for Perry to slip through. Perry jumped the stairs and darted through the door into the hall. His legs felt like straw, and his lungs were laboring to get enough oxygen to fuel this mad dash to escape.

He pounded down the hallway, thinking every moment now he would be shot. Instead, he heard Enzo thudding after him, and he knew Enzo either didn't have a gun or was afraid to risk the sound of firing.

He made it to the head of the stairs and half ran, half fell down the first flight. He was dizzy with the need for oxygen—

he'd lost both his phone and inhaler when he'd leaped for the door—and dropped to his knees on the landing.

Someone was coming up the stairs. A black shape loomed out of the gloom, towering over him. A hand like a boulder landed on his head, pushing him down, and Nick yelled, "Move a fucking muscle and I'll kill you."

"It's me," Enzo cried. "Don't shoot."

Perry wheezed, "It's…him…"

"I know it's you," Nick said, cold and steady. "One more step and you're dead."

Enzo stopped. Something metal clanged on the step. He began to cry.

* * * * *

"How did you know?" Perry asked.

It was seven o'clock on Monday morning, and they were sitting in the middle of workday traffic as they made their way home from Angel's Rest. Stop-and-going past pumpkins smashed on the roadside and bedraggled black and orange streamers. Halloween was over. Back to real life, and thank God for that.

Perry was still wrapped in Nick's jacket. He was sipping Starbucks hot chocolate and holding his inhaler, but he was fine. A little pale, a little shadowy-eyed, a little disreputable-looking under the blond stubble, but fine. Alive and well. Older and wiser.

Every time Nick thought of him making that trip through the deserted east wing and up to the tower, he felt like someone punched him in the heart. That had been too fucking close. But at the same time, he was awed by Perry's sheer guts. And not for the first time. He had to have been scared out of his wits, but somehow he'd kept it together.

"Process of elimination," Nick said. "Horace clearly believed Troy was haunting him. The Nevins weren't killers, or Horace would have been dead long ago. Duke and the girl were too young to be involved. Wynne only moved back West ten years ago. And Gilda the Great had no motive that I could see. That left Enzo."

Perry swallowed. "Thank you for coming for me." He sounded uncharacteristically subdued. As much as Nick wanted him to be more cautious in the future, he didn't like that squashed note in Perry's voice.

"I'll always come for you," he said.

Perry blushed and then offered that half-shy smile. "I'll always come for you too," he said mischievously, and it took Nick an astonished second to get the joke.

"What do you think will happen to them?" Perry asked after another mile or two of poking along past disheveled witches and windblown ghosts posted in front yards.

"I think Enzo will go to jail for whatever's left of his life. I think Sissy and Jonah will also go to jail."

"That was clever how Sissy hid her typewriter in that refurbished sewing table."

"What was really clever was Marin finding it. I think Duke will probably get off with probation. And I think Horace will relent and let him and the Savitri girl continue to live there."

"Really?" Perry asked in surprise.

Nick shrugged. "I have no idea." He threw Perry a sideways look. "What did Horace whisper to you before we left?"

Perry bit his lip.

"What?" Nick pressed.

"He said, 'One day, not too far in the future, my boy, this will all be yours.'"

"What?"

At Nick's look of horror, Perry began to laugh.

ABOUT THE AUTHOR

Author of over sixty titles of classic Male/Male fiction featuring twisty mystery, kickass adventure, and unapologetic man-on-man romance, **JOSH LANYON**'s work has been translated into eleven languages. Her FBI thriller *Fair Game* was the first Male/Male title to be published by Harlequin Mondadori, then the largest romance publisher in Italy. *Stranger on the Shore* (Harper Collins Italia) was the first M/M title to be published in print. In 2016 *Fatal Shadows* placed #5 in Japan's annual Boy Love novel list (the first and only title by a foreign author to place on the list). The Adrien English series was awarded the All Time Favorite Couple by the Goodreads M/M Romance Group.

She is an Eppie Award winner, a four-time Lambda Literary Award finalist (twice for Gay Mystery), an Edgar nominee and the first ever recipient of the Goodreads All Time Favorite M/M Author award.

Josh is married and lives in Southern California.

Find other Josh Lanyon titles at www.joshlanyon.com, and follow her on Twitter, Facebook, Goodreads, Instagram and Tumblr.

For extras and other exclusives, please join Josh on Patreon at https://www.patreon.com/joshlanyon.

ALSO BY JOSH LANYON

NOVELS

The ADRIEN ENGLISH Mysteries

Fatal Shadows • A Dangerous Thing • The Hell You Say
Death of a Pirate King • The Dark Tide
Stranger Things Have Happened • So This is Christmas

The HOLMES & MORIARITY Mysteries

Somebody Killed His Editor • All She Wrote
The Boy with the Painful Tattoo • In Other Words...Murder

The ALL'S FAIR Series

Fair Game • Fair Play • Fair Chance

The A SHOT IN THE DARK Series

This Rough Magic

The ART OF MURDER Series

The Mermaid Murders • The Monet Murders
The Magician Murders

OTHER NOVELS

The Ghost Wore Yellow Socks
Mexican Heat (with Laura Baumbach)
Strange Fortune • Come Unto These Yellow Sands
Stranger on the Shore • Winter Kill • Murder in Pastel
Jefferson Blythe, Esquire • The Curse of the Blue Scarab
Murder Takes the High Road

ALSO BY JOSH LANYON

NOVELLAS

The DANGEROUS GROUND Series

Dangerous Ground • Old Poison • Blood Heat
Dead Run • Kick Start

The I SPY Series

I Spy Something Bloody • I Spy Something Wicked
I Spy Something Christmas

The IN A DARK WOOD Series

In a Dark Wood • The Parting Glass

The DARK HORSE Series

The Dark Horse • The White Knight

The DOYLE & SPAIN Series

Snowball in Hell

The HAUNTED HEART Series

Haunted Heart Winter

The XOXO FILES Series

Mummie Dearest

ALSO BY JOSH LANYON

OTHER NOVELLAS

Cards on the Table • The Dark Farewell • The Darkling Thrush
The Dickens with Love • Don't Look Back • A Ghost of a Chance
Lovers and Other Strangers • Out of the Blue • A Vintage Affair
Lone Star (in Men Under the Mistletoe)
Green Glass Beads (in Irregulars)
Blood Red Butterfly • Everything I Know • Baby, It's Cold
A Case of Christmas • Murder Between the Pages

SHORT STORIES

A Limited Engagement • The French Have a Word for It
In Sunshine or In Shadow • Until We Meet Once More
Icecapade (in His for the Holidays) • Perfect Day • Heart Trouble
In Plain Sight • Wedding Favors • Wizard's Moon
Fade to Black • Night Watch • Plenty of Fish
The Boy Next Door • Halloween is Murder

COLLECTIONS

Short Stories (Vol. 1) • Sweet Spot (the Petit Morts)
Merry Christmas, Darling (Holiday Codas) • Christmas Waltz
(Holiday Codas 2)
I Spy...Three Novellas • Point Blank (Five Dangerous Ground Novellas)
Dark Horse, White Knight (Two Novellas)

22972520R10113

Made in the USA
San Bernardino, CA
20 January 2019